Cover Artist: Ink and Laurel

Editor: On The Same Page Editing

Formatter: Grace Elena Formatting

Dedicated to the novella sized moments, the short stories you tell at parties, the memory that feels lost until it barrels back to remind you it still exists in the present and so do you.
The ones that come and go in a blip and somehow change your life forever.

KARISSA KINWORD

playlist

chapter one

Angelo

THE BLARING of my fourth alarm was the last thing I heard before cold water hit me in the face.

"Rise and fucking shine, brother."

One of my eyes popped open, drops of liquid spilling into it, forcing me to rub the intrusion away dramatically before I had enough wherewithal to make out the silhouette of my older brother, Mateo, standing over my bed. He was all no-nonsense, black polo tucked into fitted cargo pants, a golden TechOps logo brandished across the left side of his chest. Perfectly coiffed sandy hair and a manicured five o'clock shadow across his sharp jaw. We looked alike...if you squinted.

Mateo was the version of me that cared about appearances. The one who spent fifteen years in the military and led a group of men through special operations from South America to the Middle East.

I was the dirty work coveralls, third coffee with a cigarette, sidecar on a dusty jobsite at eight a.m. version.

Mateo shook his wrist out, checking the time on his watch with his tongue in his cheek, and brandished me with another impatient glare.

Fuck. I wasn't used to punctuality. Being part owner of a construction business for the entirety of my twenties meant rolling out of bed whenever I damn well felt like it, then strolling onto a work zone to bark orders. Now that my business had evaporated, I was back to being the one who had to show up when told to and wear the clown suit. My brother was doing me a favor, I had to remember. He was taking me on with no experience to be the right-hand for his cybersecurity company, getting me out of New York and into sunny Florida, and trusting that I had the brains not to fuck it up.

Old habits die hard, as they say.

Nonetheless, a speck of guilt panged in my chest. Not enough to make me feel *bad*, but enough to wrangle a sound of defeat out of me that tapered off into a grunt of surrender.

"What the fuck is wrong with you?" The sheets slumped away as I sat straight up in the very wet, already stiff and uncomfortable spare bed at my parents' brand-new house.

Mateo placed the now-empty glass tumbler back on the bedside table and switched off the ringing alarm, tossing my phone across the room to ensure I'd have to get up and get it. "It's your first day of work. Can't be late."

"Yeah, well, my boss is an *asshole*," I enunciated, drying my face and the hair on my chest with the paper-thin pillow cases. If I didn't know any better, I'd say my parents were sending a message via linens. "How did you even get in here?"

"I have a key."

I scoffed. "*I* don't even have a key."

"That's because Mom and Pop want you gone as soon as possible, and giving you a key will send the wrong message. How is that house search coming along, by the way? Got a realtor? A list of properties? A preapproval letter?"

I whipped the sheets off and made a point to shove past Mateo on my way to retrieve my cell off the floor. He may have been my older brother, but I had a few inches and pounds on him. Not the same Army background or instinct, but when I wanted to throw someone around, I had no issues there. Thank God for years of hauling sheetrock and doing the blue-collar work that kept me physically fit despite all the pasta Ma shoved down my throat.

"Christ, Mateo," I complained. "I thought Mom was the biggest nag on the planet. You're her on steroids."

Mateo kicked open a suitcase on the floor that I'd been living out of and threw a pair of jeans and a T-shirt at me. Our parents were giving me a month in their guest room while I got on my feet and found myself a house. Which was ironic, considering for the first thirty-two years of my life in the Bronx, all they wanted me to do was stay put. It took all of six months of retirement in Coconut Creek to decide they didn't want their son down the hallway anymore.

Duran & Son went under, Mateo got married, and all of a sudden my time in New York dissipated into something pathetically underwhelming. The family relocated to Florida, and like any baby of the family, I ambled along, hoping to start fresh. New job, new house, year-round sunshine to keep me from spiraling into that November through March seasonal depression in the concrete jungle.

"You can't live in an extra room with David and Anna Duran for your entire life, Ang," Mateo said. "I know you don't step outside your comfort zone often, but I mean, you're like halfway there, bro. You've already taken the biggest leap by packing up your shit and moving down here. Think about how much more fun it will be when you have your own space, friends, a girl to come home to and bang in your own fucking house without sneaking her into the basement to avoid our mother."

"I never did that," I sneered, sniffing the armpit of the black T-shirt Mateo threw at me before tossing it over my head. "I'm a Hilton Honors Diamond member. I take my business elsewhere."

"That's a relief to hear."

"I'm going to get my shit together," I clipped. "What has it been? A week? You're asking me to have a job, start tech classes at Broward, get a realtor and a loan agent and a broad, *and* settle down. Good things take time, brother." My palm clapped down on Mateo's shoulder, shaking it. "I don't even have pants on."

Mateo brushed me off and turned on a heel, stalking toward the window and pulling up the blinds to let in the scorching morning sunlight. It was the beginning of September, but the temperatures were still stagnant around ninety degrees. Back in New York, the leaves would be morphing into the most beautiful mosaic of reds and oranges, everyone in the city breaking out their sweaters and boots, taking weekend trips upstate on the Metro North to leaf peep and hike the mountains in the Hudson Valley. There were a lot of things changing around me in a very small window of time, like reality itself. I didn't expect Mateo to understand that feeling—he'd been the director of his own destiny since he was eighteen—but he was going through changes now, too. I had this funny feeling he was taking me on like a responsibility the same way he did in the Army, compensating for life outside the military by making me one of his soldiers.

"How's Tally feeling these days?" I asked, letting myself into the ensuite bathroom and flicking on the tap. Mateo finally turned back around and his shoulders relaxed when I mentioned his wife's name. Natalia and Mateo were married in mid-June, and by the end of their honeymoon she was knocked up. They broke the news to our parents once she'd seen an OB and had an ultrasound to make sure everyone was healthy, and I swear my mother both had a stroke and saw God in the same moment. We had to peel her overjoyed, hysterical body off the tile floor and get her a cold washcloth for her forehead.

"Dealing with morning sickness like a champ," Mateo said. "Like she does everything."

"Of course," I agreed, shoving a toothbrush into my mouth and talking around it. "How is that affecting the, uh...the other business venture?"

"Don't ask questions about that," Mateo snapped, pinching the bridge of his nose. "That's not... Just fucking hurry up and get ready for work. We're already behind schedule."

A curt laugh burst out of me so quickly a dollop of sudsy toothpaste dripped down my chin. "What? You're allowed to pry into my life but I'm not allowed to check in on my sister-in-law and her breadwinning, top streaming adult fantasy nudey page?"

"Angelo." He spat my name like a cuss. "I swear to God, I don't know how Ma and Pop dealt with you for thirty-two years. I'm making it my priority to get you the fuck out of their house so they can meet their first grandchild before you drive them into an early grave."

"Are you going to tell the kid their mom and dad are famous?"

Mateo rushed for the open bathroom like he might strangle me, and another half possessed, half terrified laugh flew from my chest when I kicked the door shut just as he slammed his shoulder into the wood grain. "I'm just asking!"

Silence followed, and I spit my toothpaste into the basin and flushed cold water over my lips and chin. I was due for a shave, I noticed, staring at my reflection in the mirror. My hair was a mess of auburn-brown waves that I brushed my fingers through quickly, and then I stuck a stick of deodorant under my shirt into my armpits.

"I have a great idea," Mateo finally spoke, much too close to the other side of the door for comfort. Like he'd been planning my death three feet away and all he needed was for me to come out to execute it. "Mia."

Mia.

Shooting me in the chest might have caused less of a visceral reaction than that name did as it landed. My fingers bunched into fists on the sink top and I watched my eyes dilate in the reflection. A chill slipped down my spine, and I couldn't decide if it was a chill of fear, jest, excitement, loathing...*nerves*. Because, boy, did that fucking woman know how to get on every last one of mine.

"I'm going to call Mia," Mateo repeated. "Or I'll have Tally do it."

Death be damned, I swung the bathroom door back open and came face-to-face with my older brother and the smirk that was painted across his chiseled mug. "Don't," I said, poking him in the chest with an aggressive finger. "I don't need her."

"You do," Mateo said matter-of-factly. "She's your only hope to find somewhere to live in such a short amount of time. She's a shark, and you know it as well as I do."

"She hates my fucking guts," I barked. "Even if you asked her —which you're not going to—Mia would rather drive a Toyota Corolla for the rest of her life than be my realtor."

"Which is why it's perfect." Mateo followed me back to my suitcase as I sifted through it for a pair of socks. "She'll want you out of her hair as fast as possible. I bet that girl finds you a house in a week just to never have to see your face again."

Something about that stung. My jaw clenched and I jammed my tongue into my cheek.

Mia Russo was a multi-million-dollar real estate agent in South Florida. The younger one in a pair of twin daughters to John and Sistine Russo, though the older sister to my brother's wife, Natalia. The last time I saw Mia was at their wedding, across the marbled dance floor with a flute of champagne to her lips and a glare in her eyes that didn't quite pierce me, but instead left a blank space where you might fill in a Mad Libs adjective.

The time before that, we were in Vegas. I kissed her.

She slapped me across the face.

Hence the absolutely terrible idea my brother was presenting about hooking Mia and me up for some house hunting. As if the thought hadn't already crossed my mind in the last two months, but in comparison, I'd thrown it directly out the window. Besides, she worked with businessmen, tech moguls, investment bankers, property sharks—big money clients that kept her pockets just as deep as theirs.

In my defense, I did well for myself. I saved every dollar I'd ever made as part owner of Duran & Son, lived rent free, utilized the city subway system, and splurged on nothing outside a few drinks and a pack of Marlboro on weekends. But I didn't *look* the part. I was a fucking blue-collar boy, through and through. I wasn't what she wanted.

As a client. I wasn't what she wanted *as a client*.

"It's not gonna work," I told Mateo, stuffing my phone and wallet into my pockets and trying to escape the bedroom, leaving the conversation behind with it. "Aren't we late for work or something? Come on. Chop chop."

Mateo rounded the staircase's banister at my heels. "What, are you afraid of her? She's five foot nothing. Sure, she's got an attitude, but what do you expect from a Russo girl? She's the best in the business, and you have a family connection. You can put your differences aside for a month and get along. Your future is riding on it."

"I can handle myself. I'm not a fucking kid anymore." I whirled around, taking a breath and reasoning beyond two grown adults with a feud. "She's probably all tied up at work anyway. I'd do better with a little old lady with a realty license, not a thirty-something, high-strung, high-maintenance *boss bitch* with a vendetta against me for a party foul."

"You *kissed* her."

"It was for all the marbles!" I shouted.

Our mother materialized at the bottom of the wooden staircase holding up two identical lunch boxes with a smile on her face that rivaled the mid-swing moon. "Look at my boys, heading out for work together," she gushed. "This is what dreams are made of."

"Morning, Ma." I smiled, hiding any hint of stress from my and Mateo's conversation.

We both kissed her on the cheek, reluctantly but appreciatively grabbing our homemade lunches and hiding a sigh until we were safely out of the house and in the driveway. I opened the passenger side of Mateo's truck and there on the seat, wrapped in plastic, were two brand-new TechOps polos with my name embroidered on the chest.

Regret washed over me. Maybe I was being too harsh on

Mateo. Falling back into my old little brother antics and forgetting that we were different people now than when we were teenagers. Mateo wanted what was best for me, and I wanted to impress him. I wanted to be his right-hand man, his shoulder to lean on, the guy he could rely on when things got tough, a damn good uncle to that little baby when it arrived. He was trying to help.

"*I* won't reach out to Mia," he said, joining me in the cab. "Let's forget it and focus on the installation today. You've got a lot to learn."

No matter how hard I tried though, I couldn't forget it. Not for the ride across town, taking in the palm trees and the local businesses that were my life now. Not while my eyes glazed over as Mateo showed me code screens on the desktop at a veterinarian office we were securing. Not while we chatted about Florida sports teams and the upcoming hockey season over identical chicken cutlet sandwiches for lunch, or on the ride back home looking at for-sale signs on the front lawns of new builds.

The entire day, like a pest scratching at a wall, my thoughts kept circling back to the irritating reminder of Mia Russo.

chapter two

Mia

THE GRATE of the agent's voice sitting across from me was like nails on a chalkboard. He rapped his pen several times on the wooden conference table, enunciating each mundane, uninteresting word that left his mouth with an even more ear-splitting scrape. I schooled my face into a warm indifference. Not overtly friendly, not enough disdain to come off as a total bitch. Nonetheless, it'd become harder and harder to pretend I gave a fuck what vacation a sleazy realtor was taking after selling yet another beachfront property in South Florida.

"This time tomorrow I'll be in Turks," Burt said. He was old, and hanging onto the crown of hair circling his otherwise bald head for dear life. "Have you ever been there, Mia?"

The button extender on the neck of Burt's button-up was digging into his Adam's apple, and the pinstripe tie he wore was four inches too short, resting starkly against his protruding gut. A bead of sweat did a sad descent down his pocky cheek.

"Many times," I mustered.

My client sat beside me, ruffling through a binder of paperwork, reading the fine print on each one—the deed, the abstract, the HOA agreement, every inspection done over the duration of the lengthy process to buy his third property, this one a beautiful multi-level, mid-century modern with a home gym and private entrance for staff to enter unseen. It would go beautifully with his chateau in LA and the Upper West brownstone in New York.

Actors.

"Of course you have," Burt continued, a smug, misplaced smile on his face. "Plenty of people want to take you, I'm sure."

I shrugged. "I go anywhere I want to, whenever I feel like it."

An analog clock ticked against the silent room. Burt and his client turned their heads to their own pile of paperwork; the real estate attorney and his secretary at the head of the table fiddled through unopened emails while deciding where to order lunch; and our lender, Scott, spun idly in the chair at the opposite end.

This was my least favorite part of closing day. The fucking waiting. My heels were rubbing a blister into my pinky toe I knew would keep me from getting a pedicure for at least another week, and my twin sister Bella was blowing up my phone so steadily the vibration in my pocket was giving me morning masturbation flashbacks.

It'd been way too long since I'd felt the touch of anything other than surgical grade silicon.

I weaseled my phone out of my pocket and glanced at the notifications. Surprisingly not Bella, who wanted my head on a stick for raiding her lawyer pantsuits every time I was speaking to attorneys, but my younger, more evasive sister, Natalia.

NATALIA

Call me when you get a chance. It's important.

That's it? That's the text message after three phone calls left unanswered? She couldn't even leave a voicemail with some sort of clue into what was so pressing? I nibbled on the pointy end of my thumb nail impatiently.

Natalia was in her first trimester with my little niece or nephew. She and her husband, Mateo, married in June and had gotten right down to business. He was older, newly thirty-six, but not much older than me at thirty. They wanted a baby as soon as they could manage.

For the next most agonizing fifteen minutes of my life, I sat faking smiles in the stuffy conference room waiting to get a call from the bank, and all I could imagine was that something had gone horribly wrong. Natalia and I were close—it wasn't abnormal for her to call me and try to grab a coffee between my showings, or drop a line to vent about our out-of-touch parents— but this felt different.

Then again, if it were really that important she would have kept calling. Which meant it could wait, and my small rush of worry subsided. Only to be quickly replaced by the realization that Scott the Lender was now dialed in on me, a small grin stretching his thin mouth. He scribbled something on an empty envelope and slid it in my direction.

Free this weekend?

A sigh bubbled behind my lips and I swallowed it, instead studying the paper like it was work related. I had nearly gotten out of this closing without a scrape, without a whisper, without an awkward conversation to follow. I thought Scott would have given up on this after the first few invitations went unaccepted. Fear not, the confidence of men proved to be completely misplaced and entirely unwavering no matter how persistently they were shut down. Granted, I lead with competence first, making mild excuses to save the professional relationship we fostered from becoming unsalvageable.

I'd worked alongside Scott for the better part of three years at Branting Company. He was a private mortgage lender, who over time became a very easy contact to get a hold of, and despite his unyielding need to push our workplace friendliness into unwanted waters, he was a reliable and determined professional in his trade. Scott was good at his job, I was good at mine, we both needed one another, so therefore, there was no getting rid of him.

Scott was the exact type of man I should be interested in, on paper. He was well off, as his family were investment bankers and realty tycoons. I knew he lived in a beautiful two level on Park in South Beach even though it was just him and a stuffy little gray cat, because he'd told me several times. He was polished and well dressed, the type of man who got manicures to keep up appearances. He would, in theory, take care of me. But I wasn't vaguely turned on by the thought of him hairless and shirtless, a forgetful, boring sex life, and even more boring mornings after.

I pulled out the pen tucked behind my ear to scribble back to Scott when the phone rang on the table and the real estate attorney picked it up. Preemptively, I gathered my folders of paperwork as he hemmed and hawed for several seconds, thanking the person on the other end before hanging up and clapping his hands together. "We're funded."

A brief hoorah was followed by a chorus of handshakes and congratulations. I handed the keys of his new home over to my client and let myself off the hook, rushing through the doors onto the warm pavement outside. It was a disgustingly humid September day. The wet air licked at my arms as I pulled the oval sunglasses that were pushed into my long hair down onto my face.

I was nearly to my car, but not near enough. A deep voice beckoned me from behind, dress shoes hitting the blacktop in a jog trying to keep up with the clacking of my heels. "Mia Russo!"

"God fucking dammit," I cursed under my breath before whirling around with a cheery grin. "Hi, Scott."

He slowed to a stop beside me, catching his breath and fixing the tuft of hair that came loose from entirely too much gel at the apex of his forehead.

"Everything okay?" I asked. "Did we miss something in the paperwork? Questions? You know you can call the Branting office at any time to get a hold of me."

"You didn't let me know if you're free this weekend."

There was that persistence again.

I braced myself against the door of my BMW, crossing my arms over my chest. The hot metal scorched my exposed shoulder and I made a pained noise. Not even my car was letting me out of here unscathed.

Scott continued, "Are you ready to let me take you out for dinner yet?"

The corner of my lip twitched into a semblance of a smile. Not to be mistaken for an actual smile. It was the friendliest, most professional thing I could grind my face into at the moment. An awkward silence hung in the air. "You know how busy I am," I settled on.

"Always busy," Scott countered. "Never let yourself relax. Let *me* let *you* relax, Mia. One date, and I promise, you will be thoroughly satisfied."

"I can definitely look at my schedule for the next couple weeks and let you know," I said, dawdling with my phone as if scrolling Google Calendar. Realistically, I was willing something dire to pop up and tear me away from the conversation.

"Next Friday," he decided. "I'll pick you up at eight. Harrison's on the Bay. I won't take no for an answer."

My long fingernails dug into my underarm flesh. "Maybe."

He smirked. "Not taking a maybe either."

"Can perhaps suffice?" I squirmed. "It's hard to make plans in our field. Could have a night of writing offers and crunching numbers on the horizon."

"Say yes, Mia," he urged, leaning in ever so slightly that my skin started to stand on end. His aftershave was a musty mix of spice and fruit that reminded me of my late grandfather and his house. Like the dust from the old attic my sisters and I would hide in, playing with broken dressers and forgotten books in packed cardboard boxes. Not at all the pleasant and irresistible scent that I'm sure he was going for.

As if willed by a higher power, my phone started ringing in my hand and I drew it up between us, nearly uppercutting Scott in the chin. Natalia was on the line, a photo of the two of us from her wedding a few months ago taking up the screen. I had never loved her more than I did at that moment.

"Gotta take this," I blurted, finding the handle of the car door and wrenching it open. "My sister. She's pregnant, could be really important. Bye, Scott!" I hurtled into the driver's seat and closed myself inside the swelteringly hot sedan before he could get another word in edgewise.

Scott lingered, confused and expectant for another second before he defeatedly walked away, and I was able to let out a breath of relief. "I fucking love you," I said, answering the phone.

"Who are you and what have you done with my sister?" Natalia's voice was pinched with concern. "Is this a hostage situation? Are you safe? Say coconut if you need help."

"*Coconut?*"

"Fuck."

"Why coconut?"

"Are you safe or not?"

"I'm fine!" I shot back. "Are you?"

Natalia's drawl of disdain echoed over the receiver. "Don't scare me like that. Don't ever answer the phone and tell me you love me again or I'll assume you're seconds from death. Plane going down over the Atlantic."

"It honestly felt like it. I have a guy at work who won't take no for an answer. Your call saved me from faking a medical emergency because it's the only card I have left."

She laughed curtly. "Well you might have a real one once I tell you why I'm calling."

I smashed the power start and let out an insolent groan. My forehead rested against the steering wheel and the air conditioning shot on, blowing lukewarm air into my face. "Proceed with caution."

"I need a favor from my award-winning real estate agent sister."

"Are you finally selling that outdated pit Mateo bought as a bro shack with his roommate? Actually, are we sure they were only roommates?"

"Well, considering I'm pregnant with Mateo's child, and Frankie and Ophelia are engaged, I'd say, yes, roommates. But they are strangely co-dependent."

Natalia's now-husband used to live with his best friend from the military, Frankie. He was a nice guy—I had only met him briefly and he was clearly heterosexual—but I would take any opportunity to pass a joke about my brother-in-law. Natalia had by proxy inherited Mateo and Frankie's house when the latter moved to Colorado with his girlfriend, and she had done decently well at turning it into a boho chic vignette.

"Okay, so new house?" I said cheerily. "We can get you something closer to me, Bella, and Cami, with an extra room for your... extracurriculars."

Perhaps the most interesting anecdote about my younger sister wasn't the living arrangement, or the fact that at twenty-six she was basically a child-bride battling teen pregnancy—but the fact that she was, to put it plainly, a pornstar.

I wasn't supposed to talk about that.

"I do not need a new house," she grumbled. "And I'm on sabbatical."

"Smart," I hummed. "The belly might be a turn-off."

"It's the exact opposite."

"Men are disgusting."

"Mia, for fuck's sake," she pressed. "I need you to help someone find a place to live."

"*Okayyyy,*" I sighed out. "I'm listening. But I will say, I didn't know you had any friends."

There was a pause that made me think she'd hung up. "Well, it's not exactly a friend. Technically it's also not a favor for me, it's for Mateo. But you can't say no."

"Why's that?" One of my eyebrows shot up.

"It's Angelo."

Angelo. His name did something unpleasant to my chest. It

was tight and hot, an instant heartburn and unforgiving agita. I had all but erased that man's image from my brain in the last three months, hardly even remembering he existed except for the vague mention from Natalia. I knew the Durans had recently moved from New York down to Florida, and their mooching, lazy, crass youngest son was following them like a lost puppy—but beyond that I wouldn't let myself waste a second of mindspace on Angelo Duran.

We had the unfortunate privilege of being in the same bridal party for our siblings' wedding. Which included spending a long weekend together smooshed into the same villa in Las Vegas and competing against one another in a groomsmen versus bridesmaids scavenger hunt. A scavenger hunt that ended with that barbarian stealing a kiss from me for points on a piece of paper, and me rightfully slapping him across the face.

We avoided one another at the wedding, stealing equally venomous looks of disgust across the aisle, and that was where it should have ended. That was where it was *going* to end.

"Absolutely not," I practically growled.

Natalia sighed hard. "Remember what I said about not saying no?"

"There are caveats. There are *always* caveats," I argued. "You can't honestly expect me and that man to share the same space for an hour, let alone several hours, unsupervised. One of us would end up as crocodile food, and it wouldn't be me."

"I know you've had your differences," she said. *That's putting it lightly.* "But Angelo isn't that bad, Mia. He has a big heart, and he's a hard worker. Yes he can be a...*smidge* immature—"

I scoffed.

"But he's family."

"He's *your* family. There is no relation on this side. What would that even make us? Sibling-in-laws?"

"Sibling-in-laws!"

"I just threw up in my mouth."

"Look, I really need you here. I will never put you in this situation again. This is my big, once-in-a-lifetime favor. Do it for your pregnant sister. Or, better yet, consider it a baby shower gift. Angelo needs to move out, his parents gave him a month to find a place, but he's slow to start because he's too comfortable. Mateo has him working for TechOps now, and he just needs someone like you to light a fire under his ass," Natalia explained. "Also, considering how much you two seem to hate each other's guts, this should be the quickest sale of your life."

The sun was burning a hot circle through my closed moon-roof and warming the crown of my head. I let my neck roll back on the seat and stared off into the light blue afternoon sky, contemplating everything I'd done wrong in my life to end up in this situation. Every stolen shirt from my twin sister's closet, chewed wad of gum under a seat, blown stop sign, bad Yelp review left on a day spa. To be fair, the little artisanal soaps resembled mints in a way that begged to be eaten. That was simply a warning to others.

"He can't afford the houses I sell," I reasoned. "I have appearances to keep, and Branting is going to be pissed if I'm slumming it and the team portfolio suffers."

"Money isn't an issue," Natalia replied. "I think he might surprise you."

"Is his dick out on the internet, too?"

She blew out a short laugh. "He's frugal. He was co-owner of a contracting business for over a decade and has never had to pay rent. Plus, I'm positive Angelo has never spent more than fifteen dollars on a pair of pants."

"Obviously," I hummed, drumming my fingertips against the steering wheel. "Nat, I don't—"

"Please," she insisted.

Once upon a time, I would have ignored her pleading and gone about my day without thinking about it twice. Made up another excuse for why I couldn't help, and lied about being apologetic to get myself out of it. I was guilty of leaving my baby sister out to dry for a good chunk of our early adulthood. I was thirty now, and could admit that I was a cold bitch for the vast majority of my twenties. Something about climbing the ladder, fucking the patriarchy, stomping on the necks of my competition to get ahead and pave a path through the unforgiving jerk-offs in my male-dominated field. Until they had no choice but to respect me when I walked into a room.

My thirties were reserved for relaxation, zen. Angelo Duran was...zen-less. Not an ounce of that smart-mouthed Italian boy from the Bronx made me feel like I was on a beach in Bora Bora. More like a twelve-hour redeye with a screaming infant staring at me through the crack in the seats.

Even now, three months later, the prospect of having to work for him, see him, collaborate, and champion his wants and needs in the homebuying process made me fidget against the leather seats as if shaking off a chill.

At the same time, I felt like I owed my sister this favor. Like a goodwill token, righting me on my journey of retribution. Bringing me back onto karma's good side. After all, this may be my hardest challenge yet. If I proved to myself that I was so good at my job even a mannerless brute like Angelo could find a place under my guidance, I could do anything.

"Angelo asked for my help?"

"Yes...sure," Natalia hedged.

"Sure?"

"Your name was brought up, definitely."

"If I do this, it counts for, like, ten years of favors. I'm also off the hook for that time Cami and Bella found your vibrator and tossed it in the washing machine for the housekeeper to find." Our parents' housekeeper had mistakenly assumed it was our mother's and returned what remained of the waterlogged toy to her bedside table. I had never seen Natalia's face that specific shade of beet red.

"That was them?"

I sighed deeply. "Yeah, and I am so glad I finally got that off my chest. This cleansing-my-aura thing is great."

"So you'll do it?" she asked, pivoting. "You'll be Angelo's realtor?"

Was I actually agreeing to this? Basically confirming the next month of my life to be filled with unavoidable stress, awkward meetings, playing nice and friendly with a man I couldn't stand, and sinking down to his level out of the kindness of my heart? The old Mia was clawing her way up my throat, hissing and snarling, laughing at even entertaining the idea of it. For some unknown reason, though, the new Mia, the grown Mia, zen Mia, was pushing headfirst to say yes.

I finally put my car in drive and veered onto the palm-tree-lined boulevard, making a final decision. "Tell him I need a pre-approval letter in my email by eight in the morning or he's shit out of luck."

Mia,
Attached is the mortgage approval letter you requested. Let me know what the next step is.

Angelo Duran
COO Duran & Son

—

Angelo,
I appreciate you sending that over. Though I did request it first thing this morning and noon is considered afternoon. Unfortunately, a fake approval letter will not get us in the door of any properties, so at your earliest convenience have those numbers looked over and updated before sending that back.
Regards,

Mia Russo
Licensed Real Estate Professional
"Best of" South Florida winner
Branting Company Agent of the Year
Social media: @soldbymiarusso

—

Mia,
My apologies. Considering it's a Saturday, my assumption was that most people are enjoying their well-earned time off instead of checking emails upon opening their eyes. The letter is accurate, but thanks for double-checking. I'm sure the budget is well within the scope of possibility for this area. Let me know when you've done the work on your end.

Angelo Duran
COO Duran & Son

—

Angelo,
Well within the scope of possibility, yet not the budget I'm used to working within, so forgive me if building a list takes more time than expected. In the meantime, feel free to do your own digging and send over any listings that pique your interest. I will say, nothing in Pompano Beach specifically emulates "mother's base-ment" so you may need to think outside the box.
Kindly,

Mia Russo
Licensed Real Estate Professional
"Best of" South Florida winner
Branting Company Agent of the Year
Social media: @soldbymiarusso

—

Mia,
You're just as spirited as I remember. What an excellent quality for a woman in a staunchly male field. Reminds me of old Bessie who

worked for my father and me, nailing sheetrock until her fingernails bled. Always something to prove, good ol' Bessie.
You might benefit from trading the Birkin for a toolbelt, just to see how the other half lives.

Angelo Duran
COO Duran & Son

—

Angelo,
Which reminds me to suggest changing your signoff. It's a bit misleading. How about something more buzzy? Like: failed business owner, intern at TechOps, homeless drifter.
Sincerely,

Mia Russo
Licensed Real Estate Professional
"Best of" South Florida winner
Branting Company Agent of the Year
Social media: @soldbymiarusso

—

Mia,
Can't. I already used that for my Tinder bio. People might start connecting the dots. You, on the other hand, might benefit from someone else kissing your ass instead of kissing your own.
Who even uses a fax machine anymore?
All my love,

Angelo Duran
COO of Kiss My Ass Corp.
123 Mom's Basement Boulevard
Son of the Year since '93

—

Angelo,
This is a highly inappropriate employee-client conversation, and moving forward, I recommend that our correspondence is kept as minimal as possible.

Mia Russo
Licensed Real Estate Professional
"Best of" South Florida winner
Branting Company Agent of the Year
Social media: @soldbymiarusso

—

Mia,
Have you not gotten over Vegas yet? That was like four months ago.

Angelo Duran
COO of Kiss My Ass Corp.
123 Mom's Basement Boulevard
Son of the Year since '93

—

Angelo,
Let me know if your schedule is clear for Tuesday and I will make the necessary viewing appointments.
And no, I haven't.

Mia Russo
Licensed Real Estate Professional
"Best of" South Florida winner
Branting Company Agent of the Year

Social media: @soldbymiarusso

—

Mia,
Tuesday is open. We should probably call it a truce before then.
Wouldn't want to make this arrangement any more inconvenient
than it already is.

Angelo Duran
COO of Kiss My Ass Corp.
123 Mom's Basement Boulevard
Son of the Year since '93

—

Angelo,
Never.
See you Tuesday.

Mia Russo
Licensed Real Estate Professional
"Best of" South Florida winner
Branting Company Agent of the Year
Social media: @soldbymiarusso

———

I STILL HADN'T GOTTEN USED to the humidity in
Florida. Septembers in the Bronx could be hot, but the more
temperate, breezy fall weather snuck through more often than
not. It was something to look forward to after summers of swimming in community pools and blacktop burning the soles of your
already bald shoe soles. Back-to-school shopping hadn't come
around yet to get a new pair.

In South Florida at nine a.m., it was already creeping close to ninety degrees, and the white concrete sidewalk reflected the sun brightly enough to make my eyes water. I checked my watch—two minutes past our meeting time—and wondered if Mia was getting her revenge on me for not living up to her punctuality expectations. She would do something like that. Chess moves, always. We might have been too similar to get along, if I thought about it.

I pulled a pack of cigarettes out of the back pocket of my jeans and lit one, taking a long drag before turning toward the house we were viewing. Not much of a front yard to write home about, artificial grass landscaped nicely against spider-plant-looking bushes and flower patches, black mulch, gnome ornaments, and ceramic frog decorations lining the walking path to the wind-screen front door. An old couple probably lived here. That, or maybe a preschool teacher. Someone with time and whimsy and a fascination with *Alice in Wonderland*.

I prodded at a red-and-white windcatcher sticking out of the ground.

As a contractor, I could appreciate the little things about handiwork. I noticed things like expensive siding, gutter work, window installation, materials. This house was well loved. The owners were prideful, and that was only speaking for the exterior. I did a short walk to the backyard fence and jiggled the gate latch, testing its integrity. The AC unit on the side of the house looked new and clean. A low rumble filtered out of it, indicating it was doing its job inside, while I melted outside with a half-smoked cigarette and a bead of sweat trickling down my temple.

A car door slammed on the street, and the sound of heels clacking on asphalt brought me back to the front of the house.

Mia was rounding her silver BMW, wearing a pair of white slacks that hugged her nicely, a blue button-down tucked into the front, and a designer belt buckle at the helm. She slid her sunglasses into her hair and looked around impatiently. As if I had been the one wasting time. Admittedly, even with pursed lips and nostrils flaring, she was annoyingly pretty.

It was too bad everything else about her didn't match. There wasn't an ounce of warmth inside that little body. Not a single morsel of hospitality, nor even the ability to pretend for the sake of it.

The thing about Mia was that she would never actually go away, right? The same way I wouldn't. Our siblings were married. We would share nieces and nephews, birthday parties, and holidays, forced into one another's lives no matter how hard we tried not to be.

I was ready to put the past in the past and forget. But Mia wasn't. And if there was one thing I learned as a youngest child, second-born son, and behaviorally inept young adult—it was how to hold a grudge.

"Look who it is," I boomed, meeting Mia at the landing of the front door. "My darling real estate agent decided to show up."

She gave me a crass smile before her hand shot up to my lips, snatching the ashy cigarette and throwing it on the ground. The toe of her heel stomped it out aggressively.

"Rude," I pouted.

Even with a lift, Mia was several inches shorter than me, and with my back to the sun, my shadow totally shaded her from the blazing heat.

"Listen here, Mario. Luigi might be my brother-in-law, and the father of my niece or nephew, but that is the *only* reason I'm standing here right now. I'm doing this as a favor. So you wait for me if I need waiting on, and you stand at the door until I get here with a passcode with your hands in your pockets like a good little boy. The quicker I can get you into a house, the quicker my life can return to normal, so let's focus on that."

Mia punched a series of numbers into the front door keypad, dislodging a key and opening the door with a push.

"Normal?" I followed her inside. "Like, with your broomsticks and cauldrons and what not?" Before I could move beyond the open foyer, Mia's arm stuck out across my chest and stopped me. She pointed at my work boots, scuffed and a totally different shade of brown than they were when I bought them. The steel toe was peeking through the leather on my left foot, laces fraying and only half tied.

Mia slipped her manicured feet out of her own shoes, then waited for me to do the same. "You're in my doghouse, you bark when I tell you to. Or you can keep skipping across the hallway at your parents' place with a towel over your junk after a shower and never get laid again."

"It's never been a problem before," I assured her, hesitating to take off my shoes.

She flailed her arms. "Any day now."

Reluctantly, I pulled one foot out of my boot and then the other, revealing two completely different socks. At least there were two and neither had a hole in them, so I considered that a win.

Mia snorted, raising her eyebrows at them. "Why am I not surprised? Old cut-off T-shirts, grease-stained jeans, boots that look like they're trying to escape the feet inside them, and not even a matching pair of socks."

"Yet you show up like this," I said, stepping forward and over-shadowing her again. Her hazel eyes stayed level at my chest for a moment before lifting to meet mine. A snarl curled her lip. "Form fitted, low cut..." I bent to deeply inhale the floral scent drifting off her skin. "Perfume. Who are you trying to impress?"

"Miami would freeze over," she snapped.

Mia turned away from me abruptly, putting an ample amount of space between us. She walked farther into the house, leaving me to follow to a formal dining room, painted the same light blue as her blouse. A large, round wooden table was at the center, cushioned white chairs forming a perfect circle around it. "No funny business. I haven't forgotten about Vegas."

A small smile graced my lips. "I know you haven't."

Regardless of that entire weekend being a blur of alcohol and bright city lights, *forgetful* wasn't a word I'd ever use to describe it.

In fact, I remember the very first moment I saw Mia Russo. It was at the airport, standing outside the terminal looking for a rideshare. She was with her twin sister, Bella, and their older sister, Camilla. All of them had the same petite frame, dark hair, and matching airport casual attire. But Mia was looking around a bit dazed, not unlike me, who had never been to Vegas before. When she laughed at something Bella said, her big white smile lit up the room, and I got caught looking for a bit too long. Mia had no idea who I was, and I only recognized her from photos on social media that Natalia had posted of the four of them. So I knew they were all attractive, but knew nothing about their personalities. Stupid of me, clearly, to assume they were anything like Natalia—the younger, kinder, bubbly, excitable Russo.

What were the odds that their flight from Florida and mine from New York landed in Vegas at the same time, and we were all looking for an Uber to the same Airbnb? I chanced a wave over at Mia, who had been watching me curiously. She quickly snarled, looked away, and pointed me out to her sisters.

I assumed they recognized me now. Mateo's younger brother, his groomsman, their pseudo-family in a way. We hadn't formally met because the logistics never worked out. Mateo and Natalia dated and were engaged to be married within a year. *When you know, you know*, and all that.

A large black SUV pulled up to the curb in front of them, the driver hopping out to grab their throng of bags and I decided, stupidly, to head over and suggest we share a ride to our destination.

Mia stopped me with a pointed finger to my chest and a look of horrified indignance on her face. "Not a chance, ass-licking incel." Then she got in the car, slammed the door closed, and left me confused and mildly insulted in the rideshare parking lot.

Ass-licking incel was the most interesting, creative, unsavory thing I had ever been called. I was impressed, and also out sixty-four dollars when I had to call my own Uber. Turned out the Russos had absolutely no idea who I was, and Mia had no interest in mending the rocky beginning of our relationship when they'd figured it out.

"The kitchen is brand new, and features completely renovated white marble, all stainless-steel appliances, stove hood, double oven..." I followed Mia's voice as she rapidly fired off information about the house, sliding my fingertip across the island in the kitchen, squinting at the cracked grout. Someone else might not have noticed it, but I certainly did.

"Are you ever going to admit that you're as much at fault for Vegas as I am?" I said, stopping her before she could give me the builder's name and phone number.

"Fuck you," she answered quickly, turning back in my direction.

My eyes widened in surprise, mouth dropping into a knowing smile. Mia's arms crossed over her chest.

"Not so professional, Ms. Russo," I teased. "Not what I'd expect from Branting Company's agent of the year."

"You're insufferable."

"I'm right and you know it."

"You're a delusional hack, with the manners of an ape and the audacity of a much hotter man."

"Hotter insinuates hot." I shrugged.

Mia let out an annoyed sigh, moving once again, this time faster, into a short hallway with three doors. She pointed at one. "Bathroom." Then she indicated the other two doors in quick succession. "Bedroom, bedroom."

"You're good at this," I prodded sarcastically. "It's really apparent why you sell so many houses. Quick and to the point."

"You're not listening to me anyway." She pushed past me with a shoulder, clacking against the hardwood into another part of the house. I poked my head into both bedrooms and bathroom for curiosity's sake before rejoining her in a decent-sized laundry room that was probably the highlight of the tour.

"For your mother to come over and do your laundry." She gestured like a *Price is Right* model at the washing machine, then at a long counter beside the dryer. "For your mother to come over and fold your laundry."

I stabbed my tongue into the flesh of my cheek. "Very thoughtful."

Mia squeezed past me in the doorway again. "The basement is through that door. I don't go into basements, but feel free to take a walk down. I promise I won't lock the door behind you." She flashed a sinister smile and flipped her long brown hair over her shoulder.

"I'm good," I said, unconvinced.

"Garage for your fridge full of cheap beer." She pointed again, flipping through the thin binder she was holding. "And that should be it for this showing." The binder snapped shut, and Mia clipped back toward the front door. Every three of her steps was one of mine.

"I should be able to get this offer in by the end of the day. We can manage above, plus I know the listing agent and they owe me one, so expect an accepted offer by tomorrow, noon time, and we'll get an inspector in the door before Friday."

My head spun, the sunlight blinding me as I chased her through the foyer into the small yard and finally grabbed her elbow to twist her in my direction. "Woah, hold the fuck on."

Mia was equally stunned, looking from my fingers wrapped around her bicep to my face. Her dark eyebrows softened for the first time all afternoon.

"I hate this house," I said. "I don't want it."

Her lips parted, eyes searching mine like she'd just noticed they were green for the first time. Then abruptly, she shook herself away from me and took two steps backwards. "What do you mean you hate it? It's a house, and you need a house. Don't make this any harder than it has to be, Angelo."

"Oh, so you do know my name?"

Her lip curled, annoyed at herself for letting the front slip. "You're doing this to annoy me. I have things to do, clients to find homes for. *Real* clients, not charity cases. This is a perfect house, and if you really want to, you can always sell it—with another agent."

"God, you're such a snob, Mia. Life doesn't fucking work like that for normal people. We don't move houses around like chess pieces, or treat them like designer bags to trade and replace. Maybe you grew up with an attitude like the world revolves around you, that Daddy could buy a new house whenever he felt like it, but you need a reality check."

Her soft face turned cold and hard again. "Don't act like you know anything about me."

"No offer," I said. "Thinking I would actually want this house shows you don't know anything about me, either."

A muscle in her jaw flexed before she stomped to her car in the driveway, slinging open the door and climbing inside. Her exaggerated mannerisms and short temper might have amused me, might have even enamored me, if she wasn't such a colossal headache.

All I knew was that being in the presence of Mia Russo made me need a *fix*. A soother, a dose of something to wash her down. I slipped my pack of cigarettes out of my pocket and clapped it against my palm, then slid one between my lips. "Hey, next time you send me an address, you should do a better job," I called out at her open window. "I'm not paying you for nothing."

A slim finger flipped me the bird, and her BMW shifted into reverse. She punched the gas, keeping her eyes on me as she quickly backed out of the driveway. *Too* quickly. She cut the wheel to turn onto the main road, and before I could warn her, the sedan was colliding hard with a red fire hydrant just off the sidewalk path.

"*Shit*," I cursed, ambling toward her. A satisfied smile stretched my cheeks nonetheless; it felt wildly vindicating. She wasn't hurt, physically. Ego deaths are usually not as swift, but I made a gesture toward the sky and patted the cross hanging around my neck as I got to her door and leaned my elbows on the open window.

Mia was still sitting there, head forward, hands at ten and two, refusing to meet my eye. I blew a plume of smoke from the corner of my mouth. The taillight was shattered, red plastic littering the faux grass, her bumper crushed like a soda can. "Need me to call someone for that?"

"Fuck you," she said again, lower, softer.

"Right." I smiled, tapping her car twice and heading toward my parked truck. "Let me know when you find me a better house."

chapter four

"I DON'T THINK I've ever seen you this pissed over a man."

I glowered at my twin sister in the mirror. She was sitting on a plush stool in front of a large golden vanity in her ensuite bathroom. The scissors in my hand paused before I could square off a few strands of her blunt bob.

"I'm not *pissed over a man*," I scoffed. "That is giving entirely too much credence to the situation. I'm pissed over the *circumstances*. He's an impossible task."

"He didn't seem so bad in Nevada." Bella shrugged. "You kissed him."

I showed her the scissors in the reflection and snapped the blades together menacingly. "I slapped him."

"But would you have, if there was no one else there watching?"

"Whose side are you on?"

I busied myself with her overgrown strands of hair, clipping more aggressively and avoiding eye contact.

"I'm not on anyone's side. I'm a neutral participant in this." She was scrolling idly through her emails, sliding several directly into the trash folder without even bothering to open them.

Bella and I were similar in nothing but looks. Even nowadays, I was starting to question that. Isabella's style had always been more clean-cut and masculine, dark colors and sharp edges. She was a hell of a lawyer in the same way I was a hell of a realtor, while Camilla was a hell of a pediatric oncologist and Natalia was a hell of a performer.

Still, I kept my hair long and never bothered to hide my piercings. I'd rather wear jeans than my usual slacks or skirts, and for the most part, whenever I needed to dress up, I found myself right where I was—at Bella's house, sifting through boring courthouse power suits that always made her look incredible but somehow only managed to make me look like more of an uptight bitch. Which was fine with me. The less I gave Angelo Duran to ogle, the better.

I added some texture spray to Bella's hair and gave her a finite pat on the shoulder, helping myself to her clothing racks in the closet. "I'm so glad you chose this house," I said. "Changing the fourth bedroom into a walk-in closet was a genius move."

"Well, it was that or a nursery."

We both looked at each other knowingly, bright laughs spilling out of us in unison. Besides being outspoken against procreating given the current state of the world, Isabella had also almost exclusively dated women since law school. Something about seeing how evil and unforgiving men are in her profession turned her off of them as romantic partners.

"So, are you into him?" Bella joined me in siphoning through her clothes, pulling out a powder-pink jumpsuit with a wrap waist and holding it up for me.

"Into who?" I shook my head at the outfit.

Her eyes rolled. "Angelo."

"Ew," I spat. "Have you not been listening to a word I've said? I *loathe* Angelo. I hate everything about him. Working with him is giving me gray hairs, do you see them? It's ridiculous." I made a show of pulling my hair at the roots.

"I just think you haven't gotten laid in a while and he's not hard to look at."

"How could you possibly know if I've gotten laid or not?"

Though, she wasn't wrong. And I was now extremely concerned that I gave off starved virgin vibes at the ripe age of thirty.

"For starters, you took an Uber to my house to talk about him."

My finger shot up in protest. "I took an Uber to your house because my car is in the shop and I refuse to rent cars."

"Right, your car is in the shop because..."

"I backed into a fire hydrant."

"You were caught up in all that hate and you couldn't take your eyes off him," she deduced.

"Okay, who are you?" I huffed, abandoning her closet, now not at all interested in shopping through it. "My sister or my lawyer?"

"I'm both, dear Mia. I'm playing devil's advocate for your own good."

"I want my money back for the Uber. I came here to be vindicated, not mediated."

"You came here to complain about a construction worker who shouldn't even be on your radar. He's just a client, right? You've done this job a thousand times, found every person from every walk of life their perfect home, and never once came over to complain about the way someone smokes a cigarette on a public sidewalk."

"But the way he does it is...*annoying*."

Bella pushed me out of her bedroom into the warm, Tuscan-inspired kitchen. She slid two wine glasses off a hanging rack and opened a small wine fridge, putting a bottle of red between us. I grabbed it by the neck and uncorked it furiously.

"You're a workaholic," she said.

"So are you," I countered.

"Game recognizes game." Bella shrugged. "I know you better than anyone, and I know you're overworked, overstressed, and underfucked. Now you're in cahoots with Angelo Duran, dealing with some unfinished business there, and your body is betraying you. If you actually hate him, your brain is too sexually deprived at the moment to sort it out."

The wine cork popped and I took a deep swig straight from the bottle before filling our glasses. She might have been onto something. I couldn't remember the last time I had casual sex. Not since college, at the very least. Sure, I went on dates, but I wasn't the type to sleep with someone for the sake of it. The last guy I had been with sexually was my ex, Shane, and that was... fuck. *Two years ago.* I took another long gulp of wine.

I bowed my head, whispering, "So you're saying I'm too horny to think straight?"

"I'm saying you might not be so wound up over Angelo Duran if you were getting regular facials."

"I..." I winced. "Oh, gross, Bells."

"Think about it," she said. "He might not bother you so much if you had another guy to keep your mind off of it."

"Somehow, I bet he'd still find a way." A sigh fell from my lips.

I hated admitting that Angelo was getting under my skin. Almost as much as I hated that Bella might not be totally off in suspecting I needed to get out more and work less. It was hard for me to let myself have a break when I'd felt like my entire life was spent climbing an invisible ladder. Every time I thought I reached the top rung, it got higher and more impossible to reach. Professionally, I would always have to fight for respect, and letting myself have something as normal and personal as a relationship was somehow going to hold me back. Make me less admirable, less of a go-getter. It meant I had a weakness that could be exploited.

Not to mention Angelo was a client, and that was so wrong in so many ways.

The last time I'd actually let loose was in Vegas at Natalia's bachelorette party, during that damn scavenger hunt with the groomsmen. Look where that had gotten me.

Facing a harsh reality.

"You're the worst sister ever," I said lightly.

"I love you, too." Bella smiled. "Go on a date, get on an app, walk into a home improvement store and look really out of place in the wood section. I swear it will help."

That was easier said than done. Maybe it wasn't the best place to start, but one man did come to mind almost instantly. I was also fresh out of ideas for getting under Angelo's skin as payback for the fire hydrant, not to mention I could really skip taking an Uber from place to place if I didn't have to. It was called working smarter, not harder.

I pulled my cellphone out of my pocket and, with a twinge of excitement for the first time in forever, sent a nefarious text to Scott.

chapter five

Angelo

MIA SENT me a new listing in a link from her iPhone. No pleasantries, no signoff, just a single permalink that, for all I knew, could have been a phishing email that would infect my entire computer with a virus. I wouldn't have put it past her either. Something to make my day as inconvenient as hers had been without a car.

I didn't open it. I wasn't going to be the sorry chud that fell for something as simple as an indistinguishable link. I was taking classes at the local college for moments exactly like this one. For Mateo to ever trust me as a worker, he would have to know I was smart enough not to open the clear, obvious, credit card skimming scam.

That, or Mia just didn't want to speak to me even more so than normal after she took the bumper clean off her Beamer a few days ago. The radio silence was fine with me. Less to spike my stress levels. Every conversation with her was its own battle in a long war. Instead of satisfyingly telling her I wasn't suckered by her hoax, I sent a thumbs-up and got a scheduled showing time and date for the next afternoon in return.

Which she was late to—again.

I got to the property and did my own walk around the outside, same as the first house. This one was bigger, with seaside-blue siding and some pretty fencing for privacy from neighbors that were a bit too close, but nothing I hadn't lived with before in the Bronx. I was used to being able to smell what the people next door were eating for dinner through open windows in the warmer months.

I appreciated a neighborhood, a gated community, real grass that I could cut myself and feel somewhat grounded to homeowning. This backyard had a pool, which I'd only dreamed of as a kid, but it also dropped off into a canal. A lazy-river-esque body of water that ran like a snake through the entire neighborhood grid. Some people had put out a small dock, presumably for fishing, and a canoe or two roped against wood stakes that kept them in place. I took one look at that and returned to my truck in the driveway.

Five minutes past two o'clock now. "C'mon, Mia," I grumbled, shaking my watch back down to my side and reaching for a cigarette. I burned the tips of my fingers trying to flare a dying lighter as a car I didn't recognize pulled up and idled on the street for a moment.

Mia finally popped out of the backseat with her bag, flung her long hair over her shoulder, and the car drove away without a second look.

"Butler?" I chimed.

Her soft brown eyes rolled and she stopped a foot away from me, giving me a sardonic once-over. I wore a branded TechOps black polo and some tan chino slacks, just the way Mateo liked his business to be—forward facing. I was in the middle of a busy afternoon shadowing my brother on a security camera installation and using my lunch break to meet with Mia. Luckily, Ma had packed a sandwich that I scarfed down on the drive over.

"The car is in the shop," Mia said. Then snatched my cigarette midway to my mouth and tossed it into the road. "Gross."

I clicked my tongue. "That was brand new."

"You're welcome."

"Everyone has their vices, Mia."

"Not on my watch." She smiled in that evil, and somehow unnervingly charismatic, way that made me not as angry as I should have been.

"You could have asked me for a ride, you know? We're going to the same place. It doesn't make sense to get a cab," I offered. Like an olive branch.

"I'd rather die." Branch snapped.

She skirted past me to the front door, a warm, entirely Mia scent left in her wake. Instead of heels today she was in flats, a knee-length fitted dress, and a sweater tied over her shoulders like a shawl. She looked like a country club debutante. Simply oozing status. I admit, I watched for longer than I wanted to; it was only natural. It even crossed my mind that, perhaps in a different world, she could be worth my time. But in this one, being the bane of her existence like she was to me felt better.

"You look cute today, Mia," I said, knowing it would get under her skin in a way she couldn't combat. Kill her with kindness.

She turned around almost immediately, probably unsure she heard me right, her sharp brow pushed toward her hairline and my lips pulling upward into a sly smile. She glanced me up and down, and I might have pulled in a deep breath, puffing my chest a bit more than my posture was used to.

"You look like you're about to solicit my porch and try to sell me solar energy panels."

An unfortunate huff of amusement came from my mouth before I could tamp it down. I tried, though, clearing my throat so Mia wouldn't get the idea that she made me laugh at anything other than her sad attempts to ruin the next month of my life. In fact, I was quite enjoying this back and forth, especially after the fire hydrant debacle. There would be no coming back from that. I would use it like ammo any chance I got.

If I tripped over my own feet and landed face-first in the dirt? *Hey Mia, remember that time you drove your seventy-five-thousand-dollar car into a stationary fire hydrant? Because I do, I daydream about it. I go to bed smiling at the thought of pissing you off so much you can't even pull out of a driveway.*

Perfectly normal and healthy. I'm sure tons of men went to sleep thinking about the woman who gives them heartburn and migraines just to spite her.

Though the only other woman I'd ever dreamed about was Jessica Alba, and I can promise that wasn't out of disdain.

Mia was through the entry and into the kitchen before I could catch up. The current owners kept it coastal—maybe it was a vacation house, some place they rented out for families during the busy months of the year and were finally ready to get rid of. For the most part, that made for a clean and relatively well-put-together house. I stuck my head into a hallway bathroom off the kitchen: toilet, sink, seashells.

"What are your thoughts?" Mia was watching me curiously with a hip propped against the counter and her arms crossed over her chest.

"Do you actually want to know?"

"No. But it's my job, so there has to be some level of bullshitting I do."

I cracked out another laugh, reaching out to open the cabinets and inspect the metal hardware holding everything together. Flimsy.

The microwave was also built into the island, the perfect height for a kid to stick a head in there or shut a finger inside. That also had me thinking about the wooden stairway that led up to the second floor and the banister with spokes just wide enough for someone's noggin to go in and never come out.

"I'll let you know once I see the bedroom," I said.

Mia gave me a long, unsatisfactory scowl, but pushed away from the kitchen table and ushered me through the large living room on the way, pointing out the faux fireplace—which, firstly, made absolutely no sense from a functionality standpoint, and, secondly, had a myriad of stone cobbled intricately around the sharp ledge. Blunt force child head injury waiting to happen.

There was also a sunroom off the back of the home, a small outdoor kitchen I might care enough to take a second look at, and that damn moat of crocodiles visible through the windows all the way upstairs to the primary bedroom.

"Four bedrooms, all on the second floor. There's a home office you walked past in the front of the house that technically could be a fifth bedroom..." Mia trailed off, raising an eyebrow at me, waiting for some type of response. "I can't imagine *needing* five bedrooms, but all your imaginary friends could use their own space, I guess."

"You are on an absolute rip today, let me tell you, Mia."

Each room was relatively the same: wide-open square, walk-in closet, crown molding that needed better caulk around the edges. That was a lazy mistake owners were often too unbothered to fix. The main bedroom had its own full bathroom with a large tub beneath a window, looking out again onto that fucking death canal. How relaxing.

Mia stood beside the bed, holding a rounded post of the frame. Afternoon light bathed her soft features, washing over the wooden floorboards and showing off some scratches that again, a normal person wouldn't notice, but I did. I noticed everything, and I definitely noticed the small peaks of her nipples budding ever so slightly underneath her dress.

She wasn't wearing a bra.

Was that on purpose? Had she made the decision this morning standing in front of the mirror to slide the befitting, professional bra out from under her dress and leave it behind? Was there some other impossible reason to forgo it, besides grabbing my attention and demanding I lock on something about her that I shouldn't?

Did she want me to?

A shallow breath slid out of my mouth, and my eyes flitted from her chest back up to her face. There was a grin there that seemed to answer my question.

"Like what you see?" she tossed at me. Like an unpinned

grenade. One that, if picked up, would change this entire push-and-pull dynamic between us.

"Didn't think you would fold so easily, Mia Russo."

Her grin flattened and she waved her hands around. "I'm talking about the house."

I took a few slow steps in her direction, keeping eye contact, waiting for her to drop hers first, but she never did. "Are you sure that's what you meant?"

"Completely," she squeaked.

I deliberately let my gaze fall to the front of her dress again, pouting my lips. "I don't like it," I replied. "It's not my type."

"Not your type?" She scoffed, pushing me away from her but to no avail as I took another infringing step, nearly backing her into the mattress. "It has everything you could ever want."

"Does it?" I asked.

"And more."

"We're both still talking about the house, right?"

Mia grunted out a noise of irritation, retreating into the doorway of the bedroom. "I knew this arrangement was a bad idea the minute my sister called me."

"Why, because you hate me but for some reason can't stop flirting with me?"

"Because you're obviously only here for one thing and that's not buying a house, or we would have been done with this a week ago."

"Don't flatter yourself. Plus, those are rich words coming from the girl who chose to leave the training bra at home this morning."

"Rich words coming from the guy who noticed."

"I'm a man, Mia. I'm only so impenetrable."

It was obvious she didn't want to be near me anymore, and that observation confirmed itself when she trudged back down the stairs in a rush. I could hear her aggressively flipping through the binder the seller's agent left on the island countertop.

I took my time inspecting the rest of the upstairs, pulling the attic drop-down ladder, opening and closing closet doors, and trying to calm the weird race of my pulse and the blood rush to places it really shouldn't be. A few minutes later, I joined her.

"What do you want, Angelo?" Mia sighed, a real, tired, possibly overwhelmed sigh that said a lot more than anything else could. Being around me, working with me—it was exhausting her.

Something indifferent panged in my chest. Despite the history, I didn't want Mia to dislike me. It would be to both of our benefits if we could get along. For some reason it had never been easy, from the moment we met.

"This is not a trick question either. I'm genuinely asking you what you want," Mia continued. "A bungalow on the beach? A double-wide trailer underneath an overpass? A second-floor apartment with thin walls and terrible water pressure?"

"I want somewhere to raise a family," I said.

Mia's lips parted slightly, long fingernails paused on laminated paperwork, and her big eyes searched mine for the punch line. There was none, that was God's honest truth.

"When I find the one, that's going to be it," I added. "If I can't see my kids eating breakfast in the kitchen, or riding their bikes in the street, it's not for me. This house is beautiful, sure. I bet every single house you show me will be, but I have to be practical. There's a body of water in the backyard with God knows what amphibious animal crawling out of it at any given time. There's dangerous architecture in the living room, stone details, and the landing at the top of the stairs is entirely open. This house wasn't built for a family. Could I fix these things? Yeah, I could, but—"

"You could?" Mia muttered, somewhat in a daze. Then her back straightened like she'd surprised herself with her own voice.

"Sweetheart, I could build the entire thing from the ground up," I told her. "But we don't have that much time."

She regarded me for a moment, hesitating to give me that Russo attitude, that snarky comeback I'd conditioned myself to expect. Then she finally closed the binder, and that small movement felt like I won a battle. Like for once in my life, the thing I was saying to her actually made sense.

"When I buy a house, that's it for me," I said again. "That's where all the magic is going to happen. Twenty...thirty years from now, you'll know where to find me."

"That's fair enough," she said quietly, clearing her throat and hoisting her bag onto her shoulder.

My phone started chiming in my pocket and a text from Mateo lit up the screen.

MATEO

Lunch ended fifteen minutes ago.

"Shit." I sighed, running a hand through my hair. "I have to run. Supposed to be back at work, but my realtor got a little distracting. As she tends to."

A small smile lifted on Mia's face. I'd take that as a win too.

"Tomorrow won't work for any showings. I have class all day."

"Class?" she asked.

"Uh, yeah." I didn't know why I told her that. It was some-thing I wanted to keep mostly to myself. A thirty-two-year-old back at college learning a new trade alongside fresh-faced eighteen-year-olds? I stuck out like a sore thumb. "I'm getting a cybersecu-rity degree for work."

A flush of, dare I say, reverence passed over Mia's cheeks. She took the first few steps to the front door beside me. "You're really all in for Mateo, aren't you?"

"He's my brother, of course I am. Family is everything." I unlocked my truck in the driveway and made my way toward it. "Let me know the next time I'll be graced with Miami's most wanted realtor, or whatever you call yourself."

Mia's jaw fell open then hinged shut. There was a dark cloud rolling over the neighborhood. She looked frazzled.

"What?" I asked.

"Aren't you going to offer me a ride?"

Right, she was car-less. Completely dependent on me. What a

power trip. I could play nice, could be a gentleman, but with Mia, it seemed like the game was more than half the fun. Call it sibling rivalry, though that didn't quite feel right on the tongue.

"I specifically remember you saying you'd rather die?"

"I was being facetious, Angelo. Are you actually going to strand me here?" A pout swelled on her bottom lip. She nearly got me with it.

"Fa-what-us?" I trolled. "Try calling a fa-taxi. Maybe get a fa-ride from a fa-riend." I wiggled my fingers at her, walking backwards down the stone driveway to the truck.

"Just when I thought maybe you weren't a total asshole!" she yelled after me.

"Don't make that mistake again," I called back. "Rookie league."

It would be a lie if I said I didn't giggle a bit watching Mia disappear in my rearview mirror.

chapter six

Mia

FOR THE NEXT TWO DAYS, all I could think about was Angelo Duran. Mostly about how awful he was. Then sometimes, strangely, in line at the coffee shop drive-thru, or in the middle of a downward stroke of the razor in the shower, about anything other than that. About his carefreeness. His quirky smile and one canine tooth that was tilted slightly inward. How sunlight caught the yellow in his eyes, and how I imagined running my fingers through the bushy, but somehow kempt, beard that filled out his face. It was like I was under a spell. A fucked-up trance.

No matter how hard I came at Angelo he took the lashings in stride. Maybe he even liked them. I was starting to feel a blithe addiction to the back and forth. Our riffing came naturally, and though I felt somewhat guilty about the lack of decorum I was showing as his realtor, it was evident Angelo and I had a relationship that transcended that workplace couth.

He was my client, sure. But he was also...family. That felt obtrusively disgusting given the way I'd gotten lost in thought about the cut of muscle on his triceps for the entire humiliating Uber ride home from our previous meeting.

Maybe I was going insane.

What is it they say about proximity? Your coworker isn't hot, you're just within ten feet of them for extended periods of time?

That's what this was.

Angelo was average. A regular, tall, toned, driven, family-oriented, hands-on, complicated, *average* man.

My job was to find him a home, and I found myself shopping as if it were my own life at stake. My own children who might grow up there. No bodies of water, no main roads, no powerlines, no shady neighbors. The yard had to be big enough for a backyard playset, a family party, a dog or two. A long driveway to ride bikes and a small community—gated, safe, clubhouse access. I checked for bedrooms on the same floor, private bathrooms, and finished basements.

Something about Angelo's speech the other day had put a crack in the wall I constructed. Foundation shaken. I'd forced myself to view him unilaterally since Vegas as a smart-mouthed, distasteful, unmotivated schmuck living with his parents. That was the easiest thing for me to do, instead of giving him the benefit of the doubt or admitting I was probably attracted to him. I was beginning to see I was wrong about a lot of things when it came to Angelo Duran.

Which didn't exactly make being around him any easier. Bella had weaseled into my brain that my lack of intimacy made me feel things I shouldn't be. I had no immediate leads on that issue, but I did have a vitriolic desire to make Angelo as uncomfortable as possible, as uncomfortable as *I* was, to even the score.

And the perfect storm was brewed.

It was Friday, and we had confirmed a showing for late afternoon just outside Coconut Creek after he got off work. Scott had enthusiastically set up a lunch "date" for us when I texted him, which I profusely corrected as a meeting to nail down a budget for one of our shared clients. Afterward, I would have him drive me over to the showing with Angelo, and I would kill multiple birds with one stone.

Appeasing Scott, avoiding another rideshare, and pissing off Angelo Duran.

Scott picked me up for our lunch rendezvous and spent forty-five minutes on the patio of a stuffy French restaurant steering the conversation in every direction other than work. He spilled a generous portion of pesto escargot onto his sport coat that I thought was a bit fancy for the occasion, insisted on ordering champagne for the table, which I turned down in spades considering I was working, and then I reluctantly let him open every door for me and mansplain the interior of his Mercedes on the drive to the showing.

Scott was a good person. He would make a girl really happy someday. They would have children who played golf and wore sweater vests and probably got homeschooled. I appreciated him as a work partner, and I tried every avenue to let him down easy. Today was a slip in the mask. It was a selfish pursuit that I should have felt bad about, but upon pulling up to the for-sale sign on Sunset Cove Dr. and seeing Angelo Duran cross-legged and cross-armed leaning against the tailgate of his truck...it all felt like a necessary evil.

"So, that's your guy?" Scott gestured toward the driveway, putting his car in park at the end of the road.

"What? No," I said tersely. "He's not my guy."

"Not *your guy*," Scott corrected himself. "Your buyer. He's the construction guy?"

A flare of heat crawled up the back of my neck. "Yeah. He's an outlier. A favor for my sister. Once I get him in a house I'm basically cashing in IOUs for the rest of time."

I glanced out the passenger window at Angelo, who was very clearly staring impatiently, a small lift to his eyebrow and a tick in his jaw. He untucked his TechOps polo from his pants and a sliver of tan skin and his treasure trail peeked out from his lower stomach.

I turned back to Scott abruptly.

"Mystery that he can even afford this neighborhood," Scott noted. "What's the story?"

"He's back in school for cybersecurity at Broward at the moment, working for his older brother's company, TechOps."

"So, give him about six months before he can't afford a mort-gage payment, is what you're saying?" Scott chuffed. "I hope you had some insurance in place for this one. The blue-collar guys always think it's going to be easy, but they don't have contingency plans. Don't let him ruin your reputation at Branting Company over a favor. Your sister knows what's at stake, right? One fucked-up sale sends you back years on the totem pole in this industry."

"Right. Thanks, Scott, for that reminder," I replied sarcasti-cally, gathering my bag and my sweater and unbuckling my seat-belt. "He's not all that bad, for one. I may be impulsive, but that's never turned out badly for me in real estate. I can read a person like a book."

"Mia, don't get caught up, that's all I meant. He looks like the type of guy who catcalls you on the side of the road while he's covered in wet cement. I know that kind of guy. He sees you as an opportunity, not a realtor."

I tried not to show how offended I was. As if I hadn't spent my entire career fending off the type of men Scott was describing, the majority of them on the corporate end of things.

"I'll let you in on something, then—that's *all* men."

There was a knock on the passenger window, and Scott clicked his tongue, nodding toward it. "Right on cue."

Angelo was right outside my door, rapping his knuckle against the pane of glass. "Any day now, Mia," he said briskly.

I rolled my eyes and let out a loaded sigh. "Thanks for lunch, Scott. Duty calls."

He got out of the car, intending to come around and open my door, but Angelo beat him to it. Scott stopped reluctantly at the hood and stuck his hands in his pockets. "Keep in mind what I said, Mia."

"Will do," I answered.

"And I'll text you about dinner," he added. "We can do a bottle next time."

"*Ooh*, a *bottle*," Angelo said quietly, mockingly. He tucked his fingers into my elbow and tugged me toward the house. His touch lingered hot on my skin even after he let go, waving a hand at Scott as he drove away.

"In a rush today?" I asked.

"Just bored of watching the trust fund baby try to make a move," Angelo grunted. "Lots of lip service, and not the kind that feels good."

"You're a pig," I said weakly.

"Whatever helps you sleep at night."

"Did you actually open the link for this listing?" I said, sensing him closing in behind me while I fiddled with the code and uncovered the front door key. "I spent a ridiculous amount of time narrowing things down, and if I'm any good at my job at all, this is the winner."

Angelo's steps thudded closer, and I looked down at his work boots nearly touching the back of my heels. A smirk spread involuntarily across my face. Somehow, he carried the subtle smell of sunscreen and sawdust and beard oil that was much more noticeable with him standing at my back and a lazy breeze whispering through the palm trees.

"What was that about?" he huffed, annoyed.

"What was *what* about?" I nonchalantly pushed through the door, noticing immediately that the listing photos were a bit misleading when it came to size. The main foyer left more to be desired, and I hid a frown.

Angelo was unfazed by the floorplan specs. "Showing up here with a Suit after a date."

"It was not a date." I spun around to face him and came nose to chest, stepping on the toe of his boot and nearly knocking myself over. I pushed him back with no luck. It was like trying to push a brick wall. "It was a work meeting. Scott is a lending agent and we share clients."

"He thought that was a date."

I shrugged. "That's his problem, then. I was very clear that work was the reason for us meeting."

"Did he buy you a drink?"

"What does that matter?"

"If he bought you a drink, it was a date."

"He tried. I don't drink when I'm working."

A deep hum rumbled out of him. I could almost feel the vibration of it in his chest. I took two steps back, turning into the large dining room.

"There's recessed lighting in every room, all on dimmer switches." I demonstrated the high and low lighting options, sliding my finger over the switch. "Even the chandelier over the table."

"Is that your type?" Angelo asked. He wasn't looking at the ceiling, not even remotely interested in the fixtures and the strobe show I was putting on. "Country club, manicured, never seen a toolbox in his life, couldn't change the filter on an air conditioner?"

My tongue perused the inside of my cheek. "Are you still stuck on Scott?"

"I'm curious."

"Curious?" I asked, snidely. "Or jealous?"

"Why would I be jealous?" Angelo shot back. "You said it wasn't a date."

"So you would be if it was?"

That muscle in his jaw flared again. His nostrils, too. "Maybe I'm feeling sorry for the guy. You're a nightmare to be in the presence of, and I can only imagine what it'd be like to lock you down. You would eat him alive."

My skin flushed. The creep of heat rose in my chest, working its way up my neck. He was so rude. So flagrantly unnerving, but it did something foreign to my body. Something I hadn't felt before.

"The primary bedroom is right through here." I cleared my throat, moving quickly into the connecting hallway and then the main bedroom on the first floor with its elevated ceilings and large windows. "There's another three upstairs, three full bathrooms in total, and a half bath right outside the kitchen near the laundry room. We'll look at that next."

Angelo rested his shoulder on the doorframe, leaning uninterestedly while his eyes followed me circling the bedroom. "So he *is* your type? Maybe I've been reading you wrong this entire time."

My hands found my hips and I stared at the ceiling. Anywhere but back into his narrowed eyes, his dark brows leveling me with more seriousness than I'd ever seen from him. I replied with more bitterness than intended.

"And what if I said he was? Hm? What does that matter to you?"

"Well then I'd tell you that you're a fucking liar, Mia."

"Excuse me?"

"That's not the guy you're into. That's the guy you're using to try to throw me off. But it's not going your way."

"Is it not?" I offered, cheerily. "It seems like that's the only thing you can think about and the only thing you care to talk about, while you try to convince me that I'm the one with a grade-school crush."

Angelo pushed off the door frame and stepped in my direction. I was pinned in the corner of the room. Naturally, my eyes darted for a window or an exit strategy, but as far as I was concerned, the only way out was through him, and I'd tried that before. Unsuccessfully.

"I know girls like you. You were all over New York City. Trying to convince yourself that what you want is the Suit, the office guy, the one that's *nice* to you. But then there's a man like me that doesn't want to be nice to you, Mia. I don't want to roll over, I don't want to make it easy, and that makes you think you hate me. Maybe you do. Maybe I hate you, too."

My heart was pounding in my ears. I crossed my arms over my chest as if Angelo might be able to see it hammering behind my ribcage.

"I'm going to let you in on something," he continued, matter-of-factly. "It's not hate."

"It is," I said.

"So we'll pretend you weren't putting me on in Vegas, testing the waters, tiptoeing around something we knew we shouldn't be, until it became inconvenient for you? Too real?"

"I was drunk ninety percent of the time we were there." Which was true, but I still remembered that brush of electricity between us. That forbidden, untouchable pull. Our siblings were getting married. He was a no one, a mess, a guy I would never go for. Our lives weren't even remotely compatible. It was the booze, and the proximity, and the weird taboo of hooking up with a near stranger.

Who could have known that having Scott drop me off would be stirring up so many buried feelings?

"You teased me in Vegas the same way you're teasing me now," Angelo said bluntly. "But now, you're without an audience, so what's the play?"

I swallowed a lump in my throat. It felt like syrup dripping into my stomach cavity. Whatever was happening needed to end before I called Natalia and surrendered her brother-in-law back to his rightful owners. He wouldn't make me do it, I told myself, and I had promised to see this through. I had it under control.

"My play? Putting you in a house so that we can get past this frankly inappropriate work relationship. I've been burying myself in listings for two days to find something you might actually look twice at, but as we can see, I've failed, *again*. All you want to do is make a move on me."

"If I ever try to make a move on you, Mia, trust me, you'll know it."

There was an honesty to Angelo that made his words sound like a promise. Like I should believe everything he said without question. Like maybe not today, but someday, both of us might be on the same page.

"Can you at least let me finish the tour of the home so I don't feel like a complete and total flop?" I asked. "You can tell me every-thing you hated at the end, I'll take notes, and then we can go back to trading insulting innuendos and I can go back to my drawing board."

The facade cracked briefly, and a lightness came over Angelo's sun-kissed cheeks. "You're not a flop, Mia," he said softly. "You're getting closer."

"I am?" My voice lifted in surprise. "You actually like this one?"

He let out a loaded breath that sounded like it had been building in his body all afternoon and stretched a hand toward the hallway, signaling me to lead the way. "Give me the rest of the tour."

I was able to work us through each turn and passage of the home, skillfully addressing the architecture and the design elements. Giving my opinions on things like water treatment and the electrical grid in the area, the land and access to all major roads, shopping centers, the beaches in Pompano, airports. I was in a flow state of selling. Angelo shockingly followed along silently, providing nothing but thoughtful tilts of his head or impressed hums. It was a complete 180 from the beginning of the showing. The tension was still evident, but it had simmered to something bearable. We could, in fact, act like adults around each other—a pleasant, peaceful discovery. That didn't mean that with every quiet moment as we moved from room to room I wasn't replaying our conversation or weighing the implications of it. I assumed Angelo was in a similar state of thought.

"Have I finally cracked you?" I joked, locking the front door again, returning the key to the lock box as Angelo stepped out onto the sunny driveway. The sky was a dreamy red-orange, clouds shifting in cotton-candy formations.

"You're very good at your job, you know," he admitted. "It's easy to get sucked in when you start talking. I was wondering if real estate was actually something you liked to do or if it was just something that paid the bills, but after a full Mia Russo showing, I understand."

"Well, was construction something you loved to do or something that paid the bills?"

"Both, in a way. Something I was born to do, maybe. But I think that happens with any trade skill. I don't like staying in one place. There's a hundred different avenues in construction, and I got good at all of them. Now I'm getting good at something else. Jack of all trades."

"I interned for Branting in college. My dad has bought many properties over the years from my boss, so it was a bit of nepotism there, sure. But he couldn't buy me my position. *That* was back breaking, getting people to trust me, especially wealthy people in a place like South Florida where there's already a built-in hierarchy. I had to get really good at selling things. Really good at connecting with people, even if I didn't feel any type of connection at all. I can usually tell exactly how I should treat a client, to schmooze them into giving me their faith in homebuying. Well, most clients." I laughed at myself.

"I do trust you," Angelo replied. "I'm just stubborn like my mother and picky like my father."

"So what's the verdict on the house, then? Hit me with it, give me your worst."

"Come here." Angelo beckoned me toward him. I hesitated, sinking my teeth into the fleshy inside of my bottom lip, and then decided to go without struggle.

Angelo steered me gently by the shoulders until we were at the edge of the driveway, his chest against my back. A cold whisper of something static made me close my eyes with his voice behind my ear.

"Do you see that house down there? The white one, blue mailbox at the road?" Angelo's arm came over my shoulder to point and I stupidly noticed every sinewed vein flowing down his skin, overlapping at his wrist, disappearing into his palm.

"Yes." It was about a block away on the curve of the road. "There's no for-sale sign."

"No, because it was bought a few months ago."

I turned toward him, realizing too late he was much closer than I anticipated. Close enough to see the tinge of sunburn underneath the neckline of his shirt, realize there were several beauty marks over his Adam's apple.

"How do you know that?"

"Because my parents bought it," he said. "Good old David and Anna."

I deflated. "And let me guess," I said, "the man who's been living with his parents for three decades is suddenly worried about being too close to home?"

"I'm ready to fly the coop. Check out the other nests, spread my wings into a new age of independence."

"You could still go on long walks together."

"I want a place I can walk around naked without worrying my mother is going to knock on the door."

"Thanks for that mental picture." It should have repulsed me, but it didn't. It really didn't.

Angelo's sweet laugh echoed against my ears and made me crack a smile. I hid it horribly, twisting away from him. "So you're two hundred yards away from home but drove your truck here? It's not that hot outside."

He swiped a hand down his face, scratching the hair on his chin. "Well, I figured after last time, you might need a ride home. The least I could do."

"Wait, is that...a conscience I sense? Color me absolutely shocked. Angelo Duran, offering to do something kind? What's the catch? Where are the cameras?"

If it weren't golden hour, I might say I caught a sheen of blush coloring his ears.

"That was until you showed up with the other guy and I figured that the Catholic guilt I was feeling was actually deep internal penance I'd already answered for. Rosaries counted. I'm sure he'd love to come back and get you, so I'll just head down the old beaten path..." Angelo started toward his truck.

"Did you really drive here just to take me home?" I asked.

"I really did, and now I'm feeling like that was a beast of an undertaking, all things considered."

I hoisted my bag higher onto my shoulder. I was either about to make the biggest mistake of my life or just enough of a good one to neutralize the arrangement. It was getting chilly anyhow, sun dipping faster by the minute, and if I didn't take the ride I'd be standing idly in the driveway, binoculars watching me amusedly from the Duran house until some random man in a Tesla came to pick me up.

"Don't get any ideas." I stabbed my finger in his direction and made my way toward the passenger door of his truck. "Or I'll let myself out on the side of the highway."

"Are you into Steely Dan?" He followed me, opening the door like he had with Scott's car while I pulled myself up onto the seat.

"Is that the homeless guy who hangs out on the junction by the college?"

A resigned sigh tumbled out of him. "Maybe I'll let myself out on the side of the highway instead."

chapter seven

Angelo

MIA'S HOUSE wasn't a far drive from my parents' neighborhood. Like most places in the county, one highway ran through several towns and cities, and luckily the traffic was nothing at all like the stop-and-go grid iron in the five boroughs. I had a truck for work purposes, but the most travel I'd ever done with it was the trip I took from the Bronx down to Coconut Creek with my few boxes and my parents' old furniture I couldn't sell before the move.

Maybe she couldn't tell, but the entire car ride I was locked in on the road, hands at ten and two, avoiding any flitting looks toward the passenger seat for fear I might get caught up and veer over the median.

Mia was weaseling her way onto my skin like sunburn did. Burning and aching, overtaking, and even when I thought the worst of it was gone, my skin would start peeling off and I was stuck remembering exactly the effect of her. She lingered. She had been lingering since our last showing, and then she had the gall to show up in the car of a Suit.

It was always a fucking Suit. And the feeling in my chest when I realized it was the first moment I figured out that I didn't want any less of Mia Russo in my life. I didn't like the feeling of another guy parading her. I wanted what he had.

Somehow, that's where I found myself after two weeks of this.

The pack of cigarettes in my center console was calling my name. But Mia would hate it. So I fidgeted with the fraying seam on my jeans until, due to the grace of God, Mia pulled a pack of mint gum out of her purse and offered me a stick.

"My condo is right up here." She gestured to a short driveway, solar lights lining the loose stone walkway, large square pavers ending in front of a tall door that looked normal-sized against the two-story gray stucco. Her unit was on the end, complete with a one-car garage and a small patch of grass that looped around the side of the building. She had only a couple neighbors attached.

"Nice place," I noted, putting the truck in park. "Looks expensive."

"That it is," she said. "I have my own palm trees. Cuff and Link."

My eyebrows cinched together. There were indeed two palm trees towering at the edge of the property, but that wasn't what gave me pause. "You named your palm trees Cuff and Link? Like the turtles in *Rocky*?"

"Is it more interesting that I named the palm trees, or that I named them after two obsolete pets that got a one-second mention in a six-film mega franchise?"

My head dropped back against the seat and then lolled toward Mia. The golden streetlights were giving her dark-brown hair an auburn halo, and her already soft features were even more buttery. She was somehow that same girl giving me hell, and a totally new one in the same moment.

"I think you're an anomaly, really. Twenty minutes ago I expected to be driving you to a dungeon and tucking you into your coffin for the night."

This broke out the laugh she'd been keeping from me. It was sweet, and full. She laughed with a grin as wide as her face, and I couldn't help but mirror it.

"Are you disappointed?" she asked.

"Mildly. Now I'm curious what the inside actually looks like. Architecture is solid from out here."

"I told you it was expensive," she volleyed.

"That you did."

Mia paused, her teeth getting caught in her bottom lip, and my fingers twitched against that seam on my jeans once more. Any minute now she'd get out of the car and go home and I'd be at the mercy of a listing link until we could do this again. Whatever *this* was.

Two weeks had passed with a quickness I had been praying for but now resented.

She lifted her bag onto her lap. "Do you want to come inside?"

She might be luring me to my death. I still couldn't find a reason to say no. I only stared at her blankly as if the words that left her mouth were foreign.

"To check the architecture," she added. "No pressure."

"Right, to check the architecture," I replied. Then she was letting herself out of the passenger door, and I was floating behind her—awkwardly, at that, my hands in my pockets, not sure whether to trail close by or give her the space to change her mind and be able to play it off like I knew it was a joke all this time.

But before long, she was keying us in on a security pad and flicking on the lights in the expansive front room. I stepped onto a rug that was more expensive than anything I'd ever owned, and followed her lead as she slipped off her shoes and padded up a flight of stairs to the second floor of the condo.

"I wasn't expecting company, so don't look too closely at anything, and definitely ignore the Cheez-It crumbs on the sofa. They're a bit of a guilty pleasure of mine."

"Will do," I said, somewhat in a stupor. There were things I thought I knew about Mia Russo that vanished into thin air the moment I stepped into her space. What I thought would be cold and calculated, somewhat boring or like a veneer over an otherwise unique space, was exactly the opposite. Everything in Mia's condo was full of color. Rusted oranges and deep greens, gold, blues—so many different shades but still a perfect soliloquy. A coordinated chaos that made perfect, Mia-shaped sense.

All over the room were potted plants, creating a barrier around the one large window in the living room. Giant terracotta pots with limbs of leaves snaking parallel to the curtains, umbrellas of ferns fanning over the arms of the sofa. She had pebbled pea-looking plants folding over their hosts and spilling like waterfalls off shelves, with even more on the reclaimed wooden coffee table at the center of the colorful carpet.

Even in the shadows at the corners of the room, Mia had concocted some sort of artificial lighting situation, like a grow station of sorts for specific plants to thrive without a spot near a window.

"There's a cat somewhere, too," Mia added nonchalantly, opening her fridge and pulling out a decanter of what I assumed quickly was white wine. "Pickle Rick."

"Pickle fucking Rick," I echoed reverently. "I feel like I've entered an alternate universe."

"Why? Because you had a preconceived idea of me based on my family and my job that was more comfortable than reality?"

"I know what my brother knows and what he's gone through with your parents, for starters," I told her. My only real introduction to the Russos was a warning to stay away from the alcoholic father, and not get caught up in conversation with the mother because I would find myself in a health and wellness pyramid scheme by the end of it.

"Would you say your parents are an accurate representation of you?" Mia sipped from a tall wine glass and folded herself into a chair at the kitchen island. I pulled out the one next to her and sat down, too.

"Are we getting deep now?"

"Just a question," she added, blasé.

"In some ways, maybe." I shrugged. "Work ethic. Mindfulness. I think I know who I don't want to be because of them, and that's just as important."

She slid a glass of wine toward me.

"I thought you said you didn't drink while you were working."

"I'm off the clock, and it's Friday. I think I deserve it after a week of letdowns and no prospects in sight."

"We're close." My fingers brushed over Mia's reaching for the glass between us and she quickly pulled back, sliding her hand through the hair at the base of her neck.

A short breath of amusement split her mouth into a smile. "Two weeks ago, I would have bet money that this would be cut and dry. You'd be out of my hair in no time. Now look how far I've fallen from grace. You're in my condo, drinking my wine. It's not my proudest moment."

"I haven't taken a sip yet. I could leave right now, no harm, no foul. Send you to sleep with a clear conscience."

Mia's lips pursed. The sheen from her drink made them look wet and welcoming, and my throat was suddenly so dry I wasn't above begging for a sip. She silently tilted her head, not giving me a clear yes or no, and I made her decision for her, lifting the glass to my mouth and swallowing the sweet, dry wine.

"Riesling?"

Her eyebrows lifted. "Savant, much?"

"No, Italian."

"I've uncovered a hidden talent," she mused. "Hey, Siri? Can you play 'Dirty Work' by Steely Dan?"

"You're a crook." I laughed. "Homeless guy, huh?"

"What can I say? I keep my cards close to my chest. It suits me to be as enigmatic as possible."

Mia melted into the backdrop of her place. I hadn't seen her look more comfortable anywhere else. Even in her business casual button-down that was teetering on a dangerous tightness across her chest. One I shouldn't have noticed but couldn't keep myself from checking in on every few minutes, just in case.

"Is it common knowledge that you're Jane from *Tarzan*, living in a jungle?" I fiddled with the edge of a leaf potted in ceramic on the island in front of me.

"That one's poison," she said.

I snapped my fingers back into my palm. "What do I do?"

"Nothing." She sipped the dregs from her glass. "You have three hours or so until the points of contact turn gangrenous and eventually fall off."

"Mia, I know you're fucking with me," I said in a higher pitch than I was used to speaking, "but then again, based on our history I could be dead wrong. Your calmness is spiking my anxiety."

She giggled, humming contently, overly proud of herself. Instead of suffering in silence I lurched across the short space separating us and touched my possibly poisoned fingertips to the back of her hand.

A shocked, yet unaffected, gasp rang out. "You sick bastard."

"If I go, you go." My touch lingered on her skin, and she had yet to notice it, or yet to do anything about it.

"That's tragically Shakespearean," she pouted. "It's really too bad the leaves are only poisonous if ingested."

"Now I know your biggest secret," I said.

"There are one hundred and thirty-six species of house plant in this condo," she noted mischievously. "You know nothing, Jon Snow."

"And why exactly are there so many plants? They look great, don't get me wrong. Very Bohemian. I feel like an anteater at an all-inclusive in Cancun."

Now I slid my finger slowly across the top of her hand, boldly rubbing my coarse skin over her perfectly smooth knuckles. Mia's tongue poked out against her bottom lip and she swallowed hard.

The air was so thin between us. I was hardly touching her, but she was letting me. She was safe and relaxed in her own home, and letting me graze her skin outright. Unmistakably. Heat was working its way into unseemly parts of my body. Just from a touch.

"I like taking care of them," she said softly. "I like interior design, and the versatility that nature brings to it. Not just versatility but humanness. Real life, vibrance, color. I bought one when I closed on this condo, and then one became two and then five and..."

"One hundred and thirty-six," I finished, now trying my luck at drawing a circle around the bone on her wrist. I caught Mia's eye in the hanging low light above the island. Her cheeks had gone from a pale white to rosy, her chest a pink hue to match.

"Now I can hardly fit any in the natural light. I wasn't accounting for so many plants, obviously, when I bought this place. I had to resort to artificial and indoor grow gardens. Eventually I'll move on into a house with floor-to-ceiling windows. The more, the better."

"It's cozy," I said. "Warm, vibrant, mature. You know what you're doing. Maybe you could design my place. I'm no good at that stuff. The building? I got that. Decor?" I blew a soft raspberry through my lips.

"We said one month."

"I know what we said," I answered. My heart was steadily thudding against my chest as Mia turned her hand over, letting me spread my fingers across her palm. I repeated that same slow circle of movement from her wrist to the center of her hand, gliding suggestively back and forth, not unlike how I might touch her elsewhere.

A short tremble of breath dropped from Mia's lips and my eyes snapped to hers, half-lidded and watching my fingers roll in a figure eight pattern across her skin. "Oh, sweetheart..."

Then she snatched her arm back against her body spastically. As if I'd been a thief about to steal something and run. I let out my own huff of breath, which was muffled by the pounding of my pulse in my ears. "What's wrong?"

"We can't." She stood up with her wine glass, walked it quickly to the sink, and ran the tap, swishing water around the inside.

"Mia..."

"You're my sister's brother-in-law."

"What does that even mean?" I jeered.

"And you're my client."

"Is that in the manual?"

"It's common sense. Oh my god, I'm such an idiot." Mia whirled around with her hand on her forehead, then grabbed my glass and splashed the remaining wine into the sink.

I frowned. "I wasn't finished with that."

"This"—she gestured between us—"is not a thing. It will never be a thing."

I shrugged, tauntingly. "It was almost just a thing."

She shoved my chest, backing me toward the landing of the stairs. I let her try her hardest and stopped us at the edge.

"See, this is what I mean," she snapped. "You think playing handsy means something, and it doesn't. It was a temporary loss of cognitive function. I didn't eat lunch and that Riesling went directly to my head."

"Don't try to play this off like you're tipsy, Mia. I've seen you drunk, and that girl would have been face down, ass up the second I followed you in here."

"Ugh!" She beat at my chest again. "Get out, get out! I cannot believe I even let you in here."

"I can't believe I let you play platonic handsies with me."

She growled and steered me down the stairs to the front door, handing me my shoes and watching me balance on one foot to put them on.

"Good night, Angelo. Thank you for the ride."

"What are you so worried about?" I asked. "That it won't be a one-time thing?"

In an instant, Mia's cheeks burned scarlet again. Her little manicured fingers worried themselves with the linen material on her blouse.

"That you won't be able to go back to the Suits anymore afterward, like a good little rich girl?" I continued.

She stood there staunchly, angrily. Bloated silence filled the air all the way up to the vaulted ceilings. That was enough of an answer for me. I was satisfied with it.

Against all better judgment, I leaned down and planted a soft kiss on her tomato-red cheek, and let myself out.

chapter eight

Angelo

TWO DAYS WENT by without hearing from Mia and I started to think I might be going insane.

I spent the entire morning on Saturday lying in bed on my phone, scrolling through the @soldbymiarusso Instagram page. Some of the homes she was selling were north of twenty million dollars. Compounds on golf courses, beachfront mansions, properties with full sports court facilities attached. She was at the top of her game, and the places we'd been viewing, while grand and gorgeous by any normal standard, were nothing in comparison.

This is what Mia wanted. It's what she deserved. It's what some Suit one day would give her, and I was just fooling myself if I thought otherwise.

She was born into a life of luxury, she lived it, and now she sold it to other people just like herself. And she looked fucking beautiful while doing it.

I must have perused that page for over an hour, clicking through every professionally filmed walkthrough, listening to her chat about the specifics of each listing, watching her hips sway, her lips move, her fitted outfits hug her curves. It was a prolonged, aggressive form of torture, because beyond the sexual dry spell I'd been in since before leaving New York, it wasn't like I could just go out and get laid.

First of all, I didn't know any places around Coconut Creek, not yet anyway. I was new to town, and the time I did have had been spent with Mateo in the reception areas of insurance companies or submitting 100-level coursework on electives for my degree. Which meant I could now confidently say that college is a scam and trade schools are deeply underrated.

Secondly, the only person who could satisfy that sexual frustration deep inside me had basically told me to kick rocks. Who knows what another minute alone in Mia's condo would have amounted to? We were right there—so close, so alone, and finally seeing eye to eye. Or so it had felt. I had her on the edge of her kitchen stool, eyes glossed over, ready to let go and let God, as my mother would say.

I was ready for it, too. Unlike Mia, I was much more of a do-the-thing-and-apologize-for-it-later person. She was so worried about appearances. How bad it would be for her to get caught up with a guy like me. The fact that our siblings were married was awkward, not illegal. These were minor, insufficient reservations.

She was scared. Fine.

But now, I was obsessed.

So much so that I'd scrolled back 107 weeks on her Instagram feed before my thumb slipped swiping through a carousel of photos and I accidentally hit the red heart button to like the post.

"No, no, no, no." I jabbed the heart furiously, hitting it so many times in a panic that I disliked it, then liked it again, and had to double dislike it with shaking fingertips before I tossed my phone to the end of the bed. "You stupid fucking Yank," I groaned into the palms of my hands.

It was then I decided to spend the rest of the day trying to keep my mind off Mia Russo by any means necessary. I got out of bed, hopped in the shower, ended up staring at the wall for too long convincing myself she definitely didn't see the Instagram like, berated myself for thinking about her again, then relieved a very ill-timed hard-on because I'd already started thinking about her, so why not just get it over with?

Then I avoided going on a sightseeing day cruise with my parents around Fort Lauderdale by telling my mom I had some errands to run for Mateo, which was a lie. In actuality, I'd decided that the next best thing I could do was leave my phone at home and walk around Home Depot to focus on something else.

Only, the flush mount ceiling lights reminded me of her nipples poking holes into her dress the previous week. So instead I ventured into the garden section, and found myself imagining how the plants would look in her condo. Hanging from a macrame basket or settled high on a shelf where the sunlight could reach them. That got me thinking about her lack of space and the way she seemed almost disappointed that she couldn't find room for most of her exotic-looking leafy greens. Then I took a walk into the wood aisle; packed a cart full of two-by-fours, some rope, metal hardware, and a can of wood stain; figured everything else I needed was in a toolbox at my parents' house; and drove back.

During that time, I realized I went to the store to distract myself from Mia and all I managed to do was find her everywhere I looked.

————

"FIGURED YOU MIGHT BE OUT HERE." Mateo slid out the back door of my parents' house onto the patio where I stood bent over a table saw. One p.m. on the dot, he and his pregnant wife had clambered through the front door for a dinner that would fill all of our bellies until the next day. "Thought it would smell more like cigarette smoke than sawdust, though."

I laughed, turning off the blade and hushing the sharp sound of electrical tools to a slow whistle of birds instead. My cigarettes hadn't even left my bedroom this morning. It was Sunday, and I could smell the garlic frying in a pan on the stove through the cracked windows and my father listening to the news in a low hum behind the sizzling oils. You could take the family out of the Bronx but not the Bronx out of the family.

I wiped my hands on my discarded T-shirt hanging on a patio chair and took a swig of a half-full beer. The sun was unbelievably poignant, and my shoulders were burning despite the sunscreen Mom threw out the slider toward me to lather on earlier.

"What's this?" Mateo pointed to the pile of symmetrical pieces of wood I'd already cut, the impact gun, the wood stain, and paintbrushes still in a brown paper bag off to the side. "Mom's already got you renovating?"

Nonchalantly, I pulled a tape measure out of my back pocket and laid it across a new two-by-four, grabbed the pencil I'd tucked behind my ear, and made a scratch mark at the designated place. Then I turned the table saw back on, letting it screech to life before saying, "It's for Mia."

Mateo stepped forward after I made the cut and turned the saw back off, scratching the side of his head. "That's so funny, I thought I heard you say you're doing this for...Mia?"

I shouldn't have said anything. I regretted it instantly. Mateo followed me like a shadow as I dropped the piece of wood onto the rest and wiped my hands on my jeans this time. "I did say that," I replied.

"What is it? A jail cell? A boot for her tire? A guillotine?" He chuckled lightly. "Is it something that's going to get me in deep shit with my wife and in-laws for far longer than a month?"

"You know, I'm not as bad as I seem," I said. "She's not either."

Mateo looked at me, eyes creasing curiously. His hair was perfectly brushed into waves, short beard trimmed to frame his square jaw. He was always so put together, I couldn't help but compare us.

"What happened to hating each other's guts and wanting to kill us for even suggesting you try to get along?" Mateo asked. "Now you're building her a birdhouse like a fucking flamingo trying to attract a mate."

"It's a thank you." I ignored him, turning back to my wood

pile and organizing the pieces onto a separate table. I pulled open the can of stain and started mixing it in circles, lifting the sediment from the bottom. "I don't see the issue with that."

"The issue," Mateo said acutely, "is that I don't believe you. And I don't want to know, but I will say, whatever's going on—"

"*Nothing* is going on," I cut in.

"Whatever is going on," Mateo repeated, "needs to stop before it makes every family dinner for the rest of our lives look like a medieval incest festival."

"That's not even accurate, historically." I scratched my head. "I'm telling you, there's nothing happening with me and Mia. I wouldn't lie about that."

Nothing had happened with me and Mia, technically. Nothing more than some questionable fingertip touching. We hadn't crossed any lines, hadn't made anything awkward for the families, no confessions, no hard conversations. I felt as free as a bird. Sure, I was building her custom hanging shelves for her plants to optimize the little natural light in her condo, but that was because I saw that she needed it, and I was a man who loved helping people. Thoughtfulness should have been my middle name. It was a friendly gesture.

Any friend would have done it. Plus, it was a thank you, like I'd said. For being my realtor.

"You don't have to worry," I assured him. "Mia still can't stand me, and I wouldn't have enough time to change that if you gave me ten years. She's very intent on never letting Vegas go, and that's fine by me."

"There are hundreds of women in this town to build things for. They probably wouldn't even care about the mediocre dicking if the woodwork was smooth enough."

"You'd know all about mediocre dicking." I shoved him playfully, and Mateo gave me one back.

"My wife is pregnant. You don't know what you're talking about."

"I still can't believe she let you do that," I added with a laugh. "Poor Natalia."

"What about me?"

Mateo and I looked toward the back door at my sister-in-law with her little plump baby bump poking out against a light-green dress. She was leaning on the frame with a curved smirk, her long hair even thicker and darker than usual. She shared the same bright smile and full lips as Mia, a very similar air around her, but Natalia was cherub-like. Not as refined, not as mature, but every bit as confident.

Mateo loved Natalia in a different way, but I think I loved her just as much. And I was going to love that baby, too.

"Am I interrupting something, boys?"

"Chit-chat," Mateo replied, swaggering over to her and giving her a kiss on the head. "Work stuff."

"I had this idea to change the name of TechOps to something punchier, something that reflects the brand direction," I said. "What do you guys think about *Duran Duran*?"

"Very nostalgic," Mateo deadpanned, shaking his head. "We can workshop it."

"Your mom said dinner is ready." Tally picked up my shirt off the patio chair and threw it at my bare chest. "What are you making?'

"Birdhouse—"

"Mailbox," my brother and I announced simultaneously.

Tally glanced between us, jutting her lip out. "That's not suspicious at all."

"Mailbox—"

"Birdhouse," Mateo and I tried again, still getting it wrong.

"Whatever secret thing you're building," she said pointedly, "put your shirt on and come inside to eat. I want to hear about house hunting."

Natalia turned on a heel with Mateo, and he looked back, glaring at me in warning as they disappeared into the kitchen.

I rolled my neck, taking a deep, extinguishing breath. *House hunting? It's going great. We've been to three showings and each has gone as badly as the last. Oh, and now to boot, I'm also having deliriously realistic sexual fantasies about your sister who I am supposed to hate while I walk through the appliance section at Home Depot.*

No, that wouldn't do.

Unfortunately, Mia's hesitancy about me wasn't as far-fetched as I'd thought, and being impossibly attracted to her was a problem I really *did* have to face.

Inside, my father was in his place at the end of the long dining table, my mother to his right, while Mateo took a seat at the opposite head and Tally dropped in on his right side as well. There was a heaping bowl of still-hot spaghetti in the center of the table-cloth, enough sauce for three weeks beside it. I decided to squeeze in next to my mother, while the sixth seat at the table remained empty, noticeably. I was a very apparent fifth wheel.

"Looks great, Ma," I said, folding my napkin into my lap. My mother stood and started dishing food onto my dad's plate, as she always had, and Mateo and Natalia reached across to fill their own, which gave me a small twitch of happiness. Something so small, and yet undeniably noticeable, as Tally didn't fold into that ancient expectation of plating her husband's food, breaking the strange cultural tradition.

My mother tried to dollop a spoon of pasta onto my plate and I took over while she sat back down slowly with an eyebrow arched.

"How are things going with Mia?" Natalia asked, sprinkling a generous helping of parmesan cheese onto her pasta.

"Fine." I avoided her eyes, toiling with the salt and pepper shakers. "Still working on it."

"He saw a house right down the street a few days ago," Mom blurted. "Gorgeous place. It was this same house we're in right now, floor plan, backyard, everything."

"Right, because every house in this neighborhood is a copy

and paste, Mom. The contractors came in with a blueprint and said go fucking crazy."

"Don't swear at the table, Angelo," Dad scolded, words muffled around a forkful of food in his mouth.

"You didn't like it?" Mateo asked. I hit him with a clouded stare. As if he didn't understand the need to get far away from our parents. He left at eighteen and never came back.

"Not what I was hoping for." I stabbed a piece of meat off a serving plate, still glaring at my brother, and a smirk lifted the corner of his lip.

"Well, it's coming up on a month," Dad reminded me. "Don't be too picky. Starter home."

"There's no such thing as a starter home anymore." I huffed. "The economy is never going to work in our favor again."

"When we bought the house in the Bronx it was sixty thousand dollars," Mom said proudly. "Needed some work, but we did our best. Rome wasn't built in a day."

"You bought a house for the same price as the truck I'm driving, I don't think you can really add your two cents to this," I said bluntly. "Anyway, it's not the money. It's the principle. I don't want to settle. I've been one way my entire life, and I want to break out of that. Start doing something new."

"How are the online classes?" Mateo asked, changing the topic. "Helping at all?"

"Angelo is street smart, not book smart," Dad said.

"They're going fine." I shook my head. "It's annoying to have homework in my thirties, but the basis of understanding is there. You need me to do it, I'm going to do it. Though it's not leaving a lot of room for anything else these days between work, home, and school."

"He needs a woman," Mom pressed in a tone more giddy than I was comfortable with. "A nice Italian girl, someone to show him around town, get him out of the house. He's boring, he doesn't even play Scrabble with me anymore on the weekends."

"Don't even leave the spare room unless it's to eat or take a shit," Dad added with his attention still on his dish.

"You know I'm right here?" I jabbed. "Am I not allowed to adjust to being in a new place? I mean, for fuck's sake."

"Angelo!" Mom said sharply.

"I only got here a couple weeks ago, and I'm immediately thrust into a new job, college courses, buying a house—"

"Building things in the backyard." Mateo swept his fork wistfully toward the back door and I shot a look in his direction again.

"It is a lot," Natalia acknowledged, coming to my aid. "You're right, but your mom is also right."

Traitor.

"Maybe go out somewhere, find a watering hole or something. We can suggest some spots downtown," Natalia continued. "I have friends that would be interested."

"*Friends*," Mateo enunciated.

"Friends that I could...*find online*, in internet corners...?" I asked snidely and Nat's cheeks turned a bubblegum shade of pink.

"Find him a friend, Natalia." Mom clapped her hands. "I mean, look at this face." She pinched my bearded cheek and smacked a kiss on my skin. "He's so handsome."

"*Sooo* handsome." Mateo batted his eyelashes and I kicked his shin beneath the table.

"Enough about me." I put my hands up in a finite motion. "What are we naming this baby?"

My mother gasped, even more overjoyed with the change in subject. "Baby Anna, for a girl," she suggested.

Mateo turned to me quietly, a fake smile plastered across his face. "*Touché*, brother. I won't forget this."

"Don't hate the player, hate the game," I whispered back.

The remainder of dinner was uneventful. Natalia and my mother spent an hour listing off different, traditional, vowel-centric children's names that all sounded like the same syllables mashed together. After we ate, my mom prepped several containers of food and labeled them with sticky notes as lunch options for me and my brother to take to work for the week, and Mateo and Tally left in an understandable hurry by six p.m.

That gave me enough time of remaining sunlight to stain my wood pieces in the backyard and let them dry overnight so I could actually assemble them into something more functional for Mia. I showered, played a guilty game of Scrabble with my mother so she couldn't complain that I hadn't, and went to bed where I stared at the ceiling long enough to start overthinking.

Getting out of the house wasn't a bad idea. Meeting people, and meeting women, specifically. That would probably make the most sense for me, to shake this god-awful infatuation with a girl I would have headaches over for the rest of time. Mia wasn't the right one; she couldn't be. It didn't work that way. Who would tie the souls of two sisters to two brothers? This wasn't a fantasy novel, it was fucking South Florida in the age of Gen Alpha, where there were influencers in their cars eating twenty thousand calories in one sitting for views. Life wasn't romantic anymore.

It was a farce.

I was horny.

That was reality.

Instead of lying in scratchy sheets with my parents down the hall and a victim complex because I was assimilating at the rate of a snail, I could go do exactly what they said to do. Make friends.

And who knew the lay of the land in Coconut Creek better than Mia?

It was just a text. It was completely innocent, a way to prove that I could be cordial with Mia Russo after getting unceremoniously shot down. She probably wouldn't even answer.

That's what I was telling myself, anyway.

For the first time since our professional relationship began, I took out my phone and found her contact that had been burning a hole in my pocket since our group chat in Vegas.

ME

> Hey, it's Angelo. Had your number from Vegas. Was wondering if there's any local spots you would recommend for a beer and a burger? Figured this didn't warrant an email.

It was just about 9 o'clock on Sunday, but as soon as the text sent, a "Do Not Disturb" indicator flagged across the message screen. Well, that settled that.

Still, I stared at it for way too long, imagining she was in the mood to be disturbed, particularly by me, after Friday night. She might have kicked me out, but there was something lingering between us that begged for closure. Whether that be another slammed door, or something that would soothe us both in a different way.

I cursed under my breath, tossed my phone aside, and flew out of the boxy wool blankets. I didn't need Mia to show myself a good time. Mateo was right, there were a hundred girls that would love my wood. I just had to find them.

My teeth were brushed, a clean button-down tucked into my jeans and a splash of oil dabbed into the wiry, unkempt curls of my beard, and I was nearly out the door to drive around aimlessly searching for a bar when my phone chimed.

In one swift motion, I was plucking it off the bed and opening the text. Too quickly to be cool about it, but thankfully, there was no audience.

MIA

> Meet me at The Mackerel on Grove.

I snatched my wallet and keys and headed out the door with a dumb smile on my face.

chapter nine

Mia

I WAS without my wits when I sauntered into The Mackerel thirty minutes later. Clearly. Obviously.

Because instead of letting Angelo's text die in my message box where it should have on Do Not Disturb, I decided to answer it.

More so, I decided to meet him here, instead of sending him to a dingier, lesser food establishment so that I could make sure I never accidentally ran into him at this one.

Even on a Sunday night, it was bustling. There was a band playing soft rock music in the corner of the dimly lit space. Sailing rope and buoys hung from the wooden crown molding, and fishing net was used as some sort of nautical interior wallpaper at the helm of the booths against the wall. There were crushed and fading license plates from all fifty states decorating the backsplash of the bar, life floats and ship wheels, even a greener-than-it-should-be fish tank separating the bathrooms housing a puffer fish and a catfish, as well as several other smaller swimming friends.

The Mackerel wasn't much. It was actually a place most people avoided. I had only been introduced as a new agent with Branting because at the time, my boss was hugely interested in New England-style clam chowders and trying out as many as possible. According to him, the potato-to-clam ratio at Mackerel rivaled some of the best that he'd tried off the coast of Rhode Island.

I was confident I wasn't the only agent in my circle to be introduced to the restaurant, but likely the only one who ever came back. So while it wasn't much, it was mine. And now it was Angelo's, too. I had decided that in an off-the-cuff, unretractable way.

I sleuthed through the short, dark aisle that acted as a hallway from the front door to the back booths. Angelo was there already, sitting at the corner of the long, waxed driftwood bar with a bottle of Landshark open on a coaster in front of him. His dark button-down was tight around his arms leaning on the edge of the counter, and the yellow light of a plain bulb hanging by fishing wire above his head made his beard look auburn.

"You always know how to keep me waiting," Angelo said impishly. He pulled the chair next to him out and I sat, trying not to notice how he left his arm to linger across my backrest.

"You had the shorter ride," I reminded him. Though, I was very good at being late to things. What had kept me this time was flinging myself through my closet for an outfit that seemed like I didn't try too hard, when I had in fact tried with all my might. Something relaxed, but also sexy, that screamed uncaring when all I knew how to do was care. A shirt that showed enough skin to come off as interested, but not enough to mention it.

I thought the bootcut jeans that made my ass look like an apple and the off-the-shoulder crop top were a decent rendition.

"I'm shocked you even answered me," Angelo said.

"Almost didn't," I fibbed.

"What changed your mind?"

I crossed my legs, shifting slightly more in his direction. "I take my burger joints very seriously."

A smirk tilted Angelo's full lips. "You must be hungry, then. Invited yourself, for one."

"You texted me, remember?"

"For a recommendation," he said, waving a hand at the bartender. "Beer?"

"Yes."

"Landshark?"

"Sure," I mumbled.

Angelo gestured to his beer and put two fingers in the air. The bartender gave him a nod of approval. "You can put everything on my tab," Angelo said to him when he dropped both our sweating pale beer bottles down.

"Two surfside burgers," I added. "With some extra Mackerel sauce on the side, and a dozen boathouse wings. Tell Alfonso it's for Mia, and make them crispy."

"You got it, boss."

"Thanks, Eric."

Eric walked away but Angelo's eyes were glued to the side of my face. He leaned in slightly. "First name basis with the staff? You're more like me than you think, Mia Russo. Being a bar rat is kind of a pastime of mine."

"Don't share my secrets with anyone." I looked sternly into his soft green eyes and nearly melted. "This is a privilege not many people get."

"Why me, then? You're the queen of mixed signals, Mia. One day you hate my guts, the next you're meeting me in a ship's undercarriage of a bar, making me feel special."

We were both wondering the same things. There was a magnetism about Angelo I couldn't ignore. Convincing myself to stop things before they started was easy, but staying away, not allowing him to wiggle back in, was another story. I wanted to see him, fight with him, annoy him, flirt with him, play games. It was one of the only things that had made me feel alive in a damn long time.

When he texted me, I couldn't leave well enough alone, because it felt good to play with fire. It felt wrong and right at the same time.

"You're not the only one who needs a friend sometimes," I said, taking a long drink from my beer.

"Friend? Is that what you want from me? I don't even think you like me enough to call me your friend."

I shrugged. "We have to be something."

"Friend doesn't work for me."

"Oh, no?"

"Friends don't really meet at secret bars late on a Sunday, wearing..." He dropped his thumb that was resting against my back into the tight hem of my shirt, snapping it softly against my skin. "...this."

"Look at you," I pointed out, gesturing quickly to his jeans and tucked-in shirt. The chain on his neck glimmered in the light. "I can smell the coastal coconut aftershave."

"I never called us friends," he murmured. "The one thing I won't do is lie about whatever this is."

"Whatever this is?" I snorted. "Greasy bar food in a dive in the dark where no one can see us?"

"Except for Eric and Alfonso."

"My real friends," I snarked.

Angelo's knee pressed against mine under the lip of the bar. "At least I know that means you haven't slept with them."

"I don't shit where I eat," I said.

"No, you just bring your brother-in-law's brother there." He pressed in farther, the heat from his thigh resting hard against mine. If I were a smart woman I'd have moved it away. But I was very, very stupid, and enjoyed the pressure mounting and the tension growing. It was addicting. I liked the feeling of his strong leg dominating mine under the guise of the countertop where no one could see it. I wanted to know what it might feel like pressed into other places, like between my legs, or straddled on a soft mattress.

I drank more of my Landshark.

"Maybe this was a bad idea." I swallowed. "I don't know what I was expecting."

Angelo shook his head, a crease forming between his eyebrows as they drew together. His grip on the back of my chair tightened and the wooden knob whined beneath his calloused hand.

"What happened in Vegas?" he said. "At the wedding," he tacked on. "Why did you avoid me after everything? I know we didn't end on the best of terms but we could have at least hashed it out before now. It seems a bit overdue."

Vegas was a haze of buzzing alcohol and blurred lights to me. That, and the subtle smell of Angelo's cologne, the sound of his grainy accent overshadowing a weekend that was supposed to be entirely about my sister getting hitched.

Mateo and Natalia had a joint bachelor and bachelorette party in Sin City, and that gathering served as a long lesson that I was still learning. Angelo Duran was trouble.

The boys versus girls scavenger hunt quickly turned into a one-on-one between Angelo and me. Around every turn, we were fighting for that next point as if the bragging rights were entirely between the two of us.

Of course, with alcohol involved, the more we drank, the more the lines began to blend from black and white into a messy gray.

"You kissed me in front of everyone," I said, exasperated. "That was insane."

"You took off your clothes to ride a mechanical bull in front of everyone," he shot back. "You're not the authority on insanity."

"That was a strategic win," I boasted. "Plus, it pissed you off."

"It didn't." Angelo shrugged. "I enjoyed it more than anyone else there. Don't you remember?"

My skin flushed. A deep red that blossomed at the center of my chest and spread outward and up, prickling the exposed skin on my arms. I remembered too well. The look on his face standing at the edge of the crowd as I bobbed and weaved on the jerking animal. His glazed eyes when I slid off and met him at the exit. Angelo had grabbed me by the arm, pulled me into his chest in the loud outdoor beach club, and spoke to me like we were the only two people in the place.

If you wanted to show me how you ride, we could have done it somewhere more private.

I was aghast. He left me in the sand without a trace of amusement in his admittance, and by the time we caught up together again, the entire wedding party had moved on to a new place, a new task on the scavenger list, though my mind was still running with the events of the last. No one had ever spoken to me like that before. Unapologetically brash, unremorseful, unfazed. Angelo let me know exactly how he was feeling about me, and I was too proud to let him know I was feeling it back. Not in front of my sisters, or Mateo's other military buddies, who were more good looking than anyone I'd ever seen. That moment was the catalyst to everything happening now.

"We were playing with fire," I said to Angelo. "Natalia and Mateo were having their own pre-marital crisis. They didn't need ours, but then you went and did what you did. You had that slap coming."

"The task said to kiss a stranger," he continued, intent on bickering with me. "I met you the day before, therefore *stranger.*"

"You could have kissed anyone."

"I didn't want to kiss *anyone,*" Angelo said. He lowered his eyes to mine, searching them. His thumb had found that seam on my back again and was grazing it softly back and forth. "Still don't."

"You should," I replied unconvincingly. Our legs notched even harder against each other. My attention fell to Angelo's mouth, his pretty lips, the trimmed yet full jaw of hair mere inches from mine.

Angelo shook his head, his gaze tracing the way I involuntarily wet my lips with my tongue like I was preparing for something I wasn't sure had even registered in my brain yet.

Everything was hazy again. Apparently, that effect I'd sworn was Vegas was actually just Angelo. It wasn't the lights or the drinks or the freedom. It was his proximity. His direct influence on my prefrontal cortex.

Suddenly, kissing him didn't sound like such a bad idea.

Suddenly, kissing him was the only thing I'd ever wanted.

Eric dropped two hot plates in front of us, and my spine straightened. A deep breath I pulled through my nose ended up coughing out in a sigh of awkward relief as I turned toward our burgers on the wood bar top. "Thank you, Eric!" He left the wings between us and came back with two more beers, a swath of napkins, and a basket to discard bones.

Angelo groaned, his hand squeezing in on itself and letting go like he was holding a stress ball. "Maybe Eric doesn't want to sleep with you, but he doesn't want anyone else to."

"Some things in life are best enjoyed hot," I explained. "The surfside burger is one of them."

"They should rename it the cockblock burger," he mused.

"It's worth it."

"I highly doubt that." Angelo picked up the burger, which somehow looked small in his hands despite being a pound of meat and condiments. His first bite was messy and deliberate and I couldn't tear myself away from the show of it. A trail of Mackerel sauce dribbled down his pinky finger and he ran it through the seam of his lips, sucking the mess clean off.

My throat dried, and my tongue was suddenly thick between my teeth. "Well?"

Angelo swallowed, followed it with half the beer in his bottle, and leaned back against the tall barstool with his hands resting against his stomach. "Fuck me," he mumbled.

"Told you." A broad smile tightened my cheeks; I was vindicated.

"I'm hard right now," he grumbled. "That burger is sexual. It's touching me in all the right places."

"You're a pig," I tossed out. "I told you so, though. It's like a God-tier food snob burger."

"The cheese...what is that cheese?"

I nodded. "Gouda."

"Jesus."

"And the bacon."

"It's like the mix of the crispy and the maple with a hint of spice..." He was now dissecting the layers of his burger, looking under the bun. "What is the sauce?"

"House secret." I shrugged. "Just gotta trust it."

"This was your big plan," Angelo said. "Distract me from the fact that you asked me on a date by getting me burger drunk."

A flimsy scoff left my throat. "This is the furthest thing from a date."

"How so?"

I picked up a chicken wing, smothered in a deep orange glaze, and tore the meat off it with my teeth. "For starters, I'm stuffing my face with chicken wings. If this were a date I would have ordered a salad, an appetizer at most, something I needed a fork for."

"You're comfortable with me," he decided.

"I just don't care what you think."

Angelo took another bite of his burger and, between swallows, said, "Even better."

"Is this what it's like to live life by the seat of your pants?" I asked. "Assuming only positivity until the narrative fits what you're going for?"

"So far it's worked out for me. I'm on a date with possibly the hottest girl I've ever seen, she's insulting me—badly, we're sharing a plate of chicken wings and drinking beer, and the band is playing The Cranberries. I don't see how living life that way has steered me wrong."

"It's not a date," I said again, even less convincingly than the first time, and took a bite of my burger.

"You let me buy you a drink," Angelo pointed out. "That's your criteria, isn't it?"

Worse than being attractive, and confident, and a righteous

bastard with a smoky lilt to his syllables, he also listened. He was detail-oriented in all the ways that made it hard to ignore the fluttering in my chest.

"Maybe I'm just taking advantage of you," I said coyly. "You're clearly desperate and willing, and I'd be an idiot not to run up your bar tab. It's the least you could do after I brought you here."

"Can I ask you a question?" He pointed the fat end of a chicken drumstick at me, then dipped it into a saucer of ranch dressing. "And I want a real answer, not some bullshit, rehearsed, good girl answer."

"Haven't we been doing that?"

Angelo pulled some napkins out of the ramekin in front of us. "What's the worst that could happen?"

I averted my eyes, took another sloppy bite of my burger, and pretended it was easy to chew with an anxious lump crawling up my throat. "I don't know what you mean."

"Don't play stupid, Mia," he said directly, pushing my plate away from me. "We're past that by now. We're across the line."

I wedged my tongue into the soft inside of my cheek. "You're so full of yourself."

"You could be full of me, too."

A sharp, shocked laugh burst out of me, but the heat spinning a web in my stomach was starting to drip like honey, sending a rush of pressure to my core.

"See, this...this is what I mean," I stuttered. "The worst thing that could happen? Everything. There's not an upside to this, there's only wrong, and bad, and selfish. We don't..." I gestured wildly between us and Angelo caught my hand, laying it on the top of his thigh. "We...don't work."

"Plants in condos with no natural lighting don't work, but you find a way," he pushed.

My lips parted, then came back together like a fish looking for a drink of water. How dare he use my hobby against me? "If my plants die, it doesn't break up a family."

"If it makes you feel any better, I promise not to kill you."

"I can't say the same."

"I'm willing to die for it."

"I hate you," I said with anything other than hate in a cloyingly sweet voice.

"It's *not* hate, remember?" Angelo flexed his thigh beneath my hand, and the warmth through his jeans made me spread my fingers. His lips twitched and his gaze landed on the proximity of my touch to the zipper of his fly.

My elbow rested on the bar top, and I dropped my chin into the palm of my hand. Angelo leaned in again.

"You can't kick me out of this bar like you kicked me out of your place."

"Eric will do whatever I want," I whispered confidently. "You make one wrong move and the surfside burger will never be seen again."

"You move your hand one more inch to the left and I'll carry you out of here over my shoulder like a sheet of drywall."

There was a brief moment where I thought about testing that. But it was squashed by my name being called through the hum of the crowd and the bass guitar solo. I turned quickly, and saw Scott —lender Scott, Branting partner Scott—venturing toward our corner from the front of the bar. Of all places, of *all* people...

My stomach sank, and instantly a wall came up between Angelo and me. I pulled my hand from his lap, straightened my back against the seat, and crossed my arms over my shoulderless top. I wasn't at work, but I felt exposed as if I were. Like I'd been caught making out with a coworker in the break room.

It took Angelo a moment but he reluctantly shrank back into his own seat, as if being alone with him wasn't damning enough. The air went cold around us.

"What are the odds?" Angelo growled.

"Don't be a dick," I hissed. Scott made his way to us, his smile flatlining into a dismal curve when he realized it was Angelo beside me in the dark restaurant.

This was why it would never work. My entire life was an appearance, even the small, secret corners of it. We weren't supposed to be canoodling at the local dive on a Sunday night. I wasn't embarrassed about Angelo, it was more than that. It was something that had nothing to do with him but something inside myself that took years to get there and would probably take years to be unraveled. We didn't have that.

He was him, and I was me.

And in this moment, Mia Russo had been backed into a wall. And I didn't like that feeling.

"Little late for a home tour," Scott commented. "This is the, uh..." He pointed toward Angelo offhandedly, who had his jaw locked and his eyes narrowed. "The construction guy."

"Angelo," I confirmed nonchalantly. "Yeah, actually, our siblings are married, so..." I trailed off.

"So, you're suddenly not too busy." Scott shrugged, his nose wrinkled with distaste. "I'm surprised by you, Mia."

Angelo sat forward. "Why, because she's not interested in you?"

Scott sniffed out a lazy laugh and ignored him, resting his palm on the bar next to me. "I told you he would do this, didn't I? Blue-collar guys want one thing. I thought you were smarter than that."

"Back off, dickhead," Angelo said more sternly.

"I'm having dinner with a friend." I was flustered, and hurt, and defensive about my own autonomy. "This isn't your business, anyway, Scott. It has nothing to do with you, or us."

"I mean, it kind of does." He clicked his tongue. "We work together on a lot of funding, and I don't know if your decision-making is at its best at the moment. How do I know you're bringing in a client who can afford a loan and not just one you're fucking on the side? That's not a great partnership."

"That's low," I scoffed. "Don't stand here and insult me because you're hurt that I didn't give you a call back."

"Well, at least now I know why." Scott rapped his knuckles on the countertop and slid past my chair, stopping briefly next to Angelo. "Enjoy while you can, man. They're all the same."

Angelo moved to stand, the legs of his stool harshly scraping against the wooden floor. "Fuck you—"

"Leave it," I barked, putting my palm on his shoulder. My pulse thumped in my ears, so loudly the band was drowned out. I wasn't hungry anymore, I was nauseous. A burn of shame creeped steadily up the back of my neck and made my entire face warm and red.

"Mia, I can take care of that guy—" Angelo jabbed a thumb behind him to where Scott had disappeared.

"No, that's the fucking problem, isn't it?" I bit out. "He's right, this is my fault that I ever let it get this far. How dumb could I possibly be?"

Angelo's eyebrows stitched together. "Oh, c'mon, Mia, give it a rest. How would you have known that sleazeball would be here?"

"That's the point!" I nearly yelled. My anxiety was racing. I needed air, or an out, or to be alone in my house. "We can't be here," I said. "I *do* know better. Scott is a nobody, but look at how easily he can ruin everything for me. How quickly I'm reduced to less than because I'm here with you. Have you any idea what type of misogynistic bullshit I had to deal with to even get to where I am, just for some burgers and a shitty fucking pilsner to ruin it in an instant?"

"You're not that fucking fragile," Angelo dished back. "Stop looking for an easy way out. Pick one: Are you a cold bitch who doesn't take anyone's shit, or are you helpless? You can't have both based on what suits you best at any moment."

My lip quivered. Nostrils flared, I was glaring daggers into the dark pools of his now-lidded eyes. I grabbed my bag and rucked it up on my shoulder as I hopped out of my chair. "Fuck you." Turning away, I beelined toward the exit without a look back.

I didn't need this.

I'd let my guard down for a whole hour of my life, and it

ended up the same as last time—my heart feeling as broken as my ego, without a real reason for it. It was my own doing at this point. I was dragging the cracked pieces along in hopes the next bad decision might somehow glue it back together.

The parking lot was empty, a few cars littering the asphalt under the low street lamps. The deep bass of the band was muffled. I could hear the buzz of neon lights on the large sign for The Mackerel, a thousand gnats swarming around it.

My hair was stuck to my neck in the humidity before I even reached my car, and the band got louder as the door to the restaurant opened and heavy footsteps fell after me. I turned to look and Angelo was there.

"Go away," I groaned. "It's fucking useless."

His calloused hand wrapped around my wrist and tugged me back. One moment I was facing him, the next my spine was crushed against the driver's door of my BMW and his other hand was threading through my hair. My attention darted quickly around the empty parking lot.

"What are you doing?" I asked, more breathlessly than intended.

"Giving you a reason to hate me," he said, crashing his lips down onto mine.

The urge to fight melted away as quickly as I did. Parting my mouth, I opened to Angelo's kiss, letting myself fall into it. My arms wrapped around his neck, and it only got deeper and more desperate as his tongue danced across mine and his fingers clutched pleasurably against my scalp. I was kissing him, and unlike the first time, I wasn't worried about the people around us. The looks, the guilt—I didn't have to pretend like I wasn't enjoying every second of his soft lips, his strong body holding me captive against my car. Angelo's thigh pressed between mine, his knee catching at the apex of my jeans, and I let out a soft hum of approval. Angelo's mouth crested into a wide smile against my lips.

"You're driving me crazy," he mumbled. His breath was sweet, and his lips skated down my jaw, to the skin beneath my ear. He pressed a kiss to my exposed collarbone and I dropped my head back against the roof of the car.

"We should stop," I gasped.

"No." He kissed me again. This time, his hand in my hair dragged down my throat to my chest. His thumb grazed the sensitive bud of my breast and kept going, finally stopping at the button on my jeans.

Protest lodged in my throat, my breaths were coming in bursts, and I realized I'd started to cant my hips against his leg all on my own. The feeling was unbelievable, pleasure pooling between my thighs.

The door to the bar opened again and two people filed out. I hid my face in the crook of Angelo's neck.

"They can't see us," he promised. His voice was low and the hint of his accent was entirely gone, replaced with the drawl of something more deep and tortured.

"That doesn't make it any better," I replied.

The button of my jeans popped open under Angelo's precise fingers. Then the zipper fell with it. His eyes bore into mine, searching, waiting, and I was too overwhelmed to do anything but let it happen. Once he realized I wasn't going to tell him to stop again, Angelo trailed his fingertips into the front of my jeans, and curled them in a way that made stars pass in my vision.

"Is *this* better?" he asked.

My eyes shuttered closed as he touched me, a long finger drawing circles around my clit. It was methodic, soft, the perfect amount of teasing to have me chasing the pressure every time he pulled away.

I hated how good it felt. I hated how much I didn't hate it at all.

"It's pretty good," I managed.

Our lips came together again. This time, his hum of satisfaction was loud. I felt it in my chest—the vibration, the *need*. He was hard against my leg, the outline of his cock pressing firmly against his tight jeans.

"Is touching you here the only way to get you to be nice to me, Mia?"

His fingers moved faster, harder. A cloud of lust had overtaken me, and I was losing my ability to think about anything outside of the rush of pleasure reaching its peak, Angelo's dark voice in my ear, his small groans of satisfaction accompanying each of my soft whimpers.

"Maybe," I breathed. "Yes."

"That's it, Mia, girl. Soak me in all that hate." I clutched Angelo's forearm and my nails sank deep into his skin as he slid a finger inside of me.

"*Ohmygod.*" The words came out bunched together as an orgasm crashed through me. My legs tightened; my core shook. I was in a trance and the only thing in my entire world was Angelo. Him and me and this euphoric moment.

We weren't at a bar together that we shouldn't be at, in a parking lot we shouldn't be in, doing a thing we definitely shouldn't be doing...until we were. Until reality came back into focus and my high softened, and Angelo was watching me with reverence as I learned how to breathe on my own again.

He slid his finger from inside me, and the ache of the loss made me sigh. Then he brought that same finger that had just worked me to a climax to his lips and made me watch as he licked it clean.

"That kiss went a lot better than the first one," he said. "Makes me want to try again."

"I..." I pulled my zipper up, buttoning my jeans. "That..."

"I know." Angelo brushed a strand of hair behind my ear. "Can never happen again."

"Right." I swallowed, unhappy with that.

What is wrong with you, Mia?

Angelo adjusted himself very deliberately, and my cheeks flamed at the thought of him still erect, hurting, wanting for relief. I imagined him going back home and getting himself off, and another wave of need punched into my lower belly. He seemed very content with himself, though. Like he'd done everything he'd set out to do. Like he'd won an invisible contest.

The sky was speckled with stars, and a cooler September breeze was gusting through the parking lot. I shivered as the cold air blanketed me and Angelo ran a hand down my goose-pebbled arm.

"Got your car back," he noted, pulling open the driver's door. I stepped around it. "Are you good to drive yourself home?"

"Where are you going to go?" I asked.

"Well, I still have a tab to settle inside. I went chasing a girl out the door without my credit card."

A laugh bubbled out of me. "That was stupid of you."

He leaned in, flashing a proud smile. "It's not the first time."

I dropped into my car and Angelo closed the door behind me, leaning through the open window when I rolled it down. "There's no fire hydrants in the immediate vicinity," he said. "There is, however, a street lamp with a concrete base about twenty feet to your right, so try to cut the wheel sooner rather than later."

"You're still an ass." I scrunched my nose at him. "Do me a favor, keep The Mackerel between us."

"This entire night," he said. "Our little secret."

"Don't make me regret this."

He saluted me, backing a safe distance away from my car. "Do you like me yet?"

"No," I answered plainly. "But you definitely liked one of my Instagram posts from 107 weeks ago yesterday."

Angelo's smile caved. He slid his fingers through the hair at the nape of his neck and scratched it nervously. "Must have been a glitch."

I didn't believe him, but when I got home, I was in a lighter mood. My soul was less exhausted, and the pressure that was perpetually at the back of my skull had subsided. Maybe Bella deserved a phone call. Not to tell her that Angelo had done what needed to be done—God, no—but that I'd wielded her advice and hooked up with someone and now I was Dorothy in Oz, seeing in technicolor.

Tomorrow.

Tomorrow, I could answer for my crimes. Right now, I was floating in them.

chapter ten

Mia

MONDAY MORNING, I had a full staff meeting in the Branting office in Miami. We operated all over Florida and had offices in New York, Los Angeles, Dallas, and Chicago, to name a few.

Mr. Branting himself was at the head of our long oak conference table, at the top of a tower overlooking the bright, vital city and the most beautiful ocean on the East Coast.

We were zeroing in on the end of Q3, and the incentives for the approaching end of the fiscal year were on every single agent's mind. Who was going to make the top agent? Who was getting dropped for inability to reach quotas? Branting was a sought-after landing zone for young realtors trying to reach a peak in their careers. The prestige of being with our office spoke for itself—we didn't lose. If there was property or multi-million-dollar listings to be sold, we were the company that got that first call. We were trusted, innovative, and ever-changing with the highs and lows of quite possibly the hardest economic housing market in twenty years.

I wasn't worried about myself. My sales spoke more than I ever had to. I had worked so hard that people were scraping to catch up with me, which was one of the reasons I'd even been open to taking Angelo on as a client for the month of September.

For two hours, I listened to a numbers report from our accountant as she went from top to bottom of our agency and several other branches. Mr. Branting tapped his pen periodically against the table or his chin, sometimes flicking it in impressive circles around his fingers like a drummer with a drumstick. At the helm of the room was a large screen with a Zoom conference hosting the branch team's principal broker, management associates, and agents.

Usually, I would brownnose. Take notes, make myself look busy and interested, all while the other men would twiddle their thumbs indifferently, boredly. I thought I had to be the one making a concerted effort.

Today, though, my mind was everywhere but in the meeting. It was still pressed against my car. Sweating from the humidity, and the heat between Angelo and me. It was reliving the moment his fingers breached my cotton panties, delicately exploring flesh that hadn't been touched in God knew how long. I could still feel him when I got lost enough in my daydream. His whispers, the broken breathing, the way I knew he was as affected as I was but didn't care to do anything but satisfy me.

By lunch time, there was no coming back from it. We took a break for an hour, and I obsessively checked my phone thinking there would be a text, or at least some type of correspondence. How could he not say anything after that? I was wearing myself into a mania over one spirited dalliance in a dive bar parking lot like it was the epitome of romance. But for me, it *sort of* had been. I didn't know any differently. I wasn't dating around. I was focusing on my career, the way a Russo girl was raised to do.

Angelo had tried harder for me than any man I'd ever met. He made me feel wanted. Despite the challenge, and the insolence, the attitude, how I fought him at every turn. That meant he saw something *more* in me. He saw me in a light I didn't pass through, a way I didn't press to be seen.

Beyond the physical moment we had, I was starting to think I would miss Angelo when the house hunt was over. I'd miss him as a conversationalist, a comedian, as a break in my hard work week otherwise. Being around him was easy.

But we couldn't be friends. *Friends* wasn't going to happen.

Branting let us off the hook mid-afternoon after surprisingly only firing three agents from the company. I had an inkling that his mood booster was from finalizing his second divorce and the twenty-three-year-old he was now dating. That was none of my business and I had no reason to complain about an early Monday. It gave me time to walk downtown in Miami, enjoy the breeze, clear my head, and find the absolute most adorable baby clothing boutique.

After spending several hundred dollars on neutral clothing and toys for my future niece or nephew, I drove back to Coconut Creek, directly to Natalia and Mateo's house to share my findings with my sister.

She was at home nesting while her husband was still at work.

"You know I'm only sixteen weeks pregnant, right? Hardly in my second trimester."

"Don't tell me when to spoil my baby," I schmoozed. I followed Natalia into what would eventually be the nursery with the massive bag of clothes. The room was cleared out, with only a rogue dresser against one wall that I believed once belonged to Mateo's best friend, Frankie, and a pile of paint swatches and wall-paper samples on top of it.

I helped myself to the samples, holding them against each other in the shadows of the room, and then again in an area where the light from the window hit the wall. "Can I design it?" I asked.

"The nursery?" She seemed surprised. "You really want to?"

"Yeah, I'd love that. My own little gift to the baby, a piece of Auntie Mia every day." I spun in a circle, making framing motions with my fingers. "Crib over against the far wall, a fun accent wall-paper. We could even divide the room with paneling for some texture."

"I'm married to the idea of it being neutral either way," she hummed. "Pop of color, some fun thrifted frames. A room they can grow into rather than out of in a couple years."

"Say no more," I said. "My brain is a churning wheel that you have watered."

Natalia snorted, sorting through the large trough of baby clothes, pulling each item out wistfully and puckering her bottom lip. One particular light-brown cardigan with a teddy bear peeking out of the pocket earned a sniffle as she hugged it tightly to her chest.

"Aren't these tiny diaper covers precious?" I unfolded them, wiggling the blooming, ruffled tushies. "And can never have enough sun hats." There were a handful of bucket-style hats with chin straps that I knew would be a no-brainer given the Florida UV index and the amount of time this spoiled child would spend on a beach.

"These are only some small things," I added. "When we know the gender I'll obviously have to go shopping again."

Natalia crossed her arms over her chest and leaned against the old dresser with a jovial smile on her face. "There's something different about you."

My head tilted. "What do you mean?"

"You're acting weird."

"Okay," I huffed. "That's the last time I come bearing gifts and offering my interior design services pro bono."

"No, it's not that." Natalia waved me off. "You're...happy? Don't take that the wrong way." She flailed her hand again and my eyebrow arched. "It's just that you're always in one mood. Like, sarcastic sycophant girl boss. But, right now I'm sensing a carefree, artsy, creative nymph."

"What am I, a Spotify Daylist?"

She snapped her fingers, a bigger grin stretching across her glowing cheeks. "I know."

"What?"

"You're seeing someone."

I scoffed, but a shy warmth sprouted at the base of my neck. "No, I'm not."

"Liar," she said cheerfully. "Spill it, right now. I can't believe you didn't bring this up sooner."

I pulled a deep breath into my chest and avoided Natalia's gleeful stare and shimmering eyes as I left the in-progress nursery and padded back into the main area of the house. She cornered me at the kitchen island.

"There is only one good reason for a mood like the one you're in right now, and that means you've been having sex."

If that was the vibe I was giving off, then I might turn into an actual ball of sunshine after intercourse. Mother Theresa-level sainthood.

"I *promise* you that is not the case," I swore.

"What's his name?"

I shook my head, snorting out a laugh.

"Is he one of the guys you work with? Big money maker, Agent Suave? Are you guys taking over the real estate market together?"

"God, you are such an annoying little sister. It's almost like we still live at home."

"You don't want to bring him around yet because it's new, I get it, it's fine."

My eyes rolled contemptuously, but I was amused, and slightly embarrassed. And I wished like hell I could actually be honest with my sister about what was going on, because talking it out with someone might be the one thing that could keep me sane.

"Tell Mr. Realtor that you're on the market, so he better lock it down before offers start lining up."

"Are you having fun?" I mused. "Has your own job been that boring lately?"

"Self-imposed furlough is torture. What am I supposed to do all day? Clean?"

Before the pregnancy, Natalia was running one of the most successful independent adult content pages on the internet. She still did, with the catalogue she'd built alongside Mateo. My older sisters and I were sworn to secrecy about their salacious extracurricular business ventures, and only a handful of people knew, one of them being Angelo.

"Maybe you *could* help me with something." I bit at the tip of my thumbnail hesitantly. "Say there *was* sex..."

Natalia lit up like a firework on the Fourth of July. "I knew it!"

I lifted a finger to shush her and she sucked her lips into her mouth. "What is...something that men go crazy for?" I asked, feeling a rush of shame and awkwardness, but Natalia's face was rife with excitement.

"Use two hands." She smiled.

"Two..." I held my fists up, one on top of each other. "Two hands?"

"Mm-hmm."

"What if there isn't two hands' worth?"

Natalia blinked rapidly.

The image of Angelo's erection pressed against the seam of his jeans came to mind, and I realized that I likely wouldn't run into that issue. I might need three hands, actually.

"Never mind," I said quickly.

Between us on the island, my phone lit up, vibrating with a text message. At first glance, I saw Angelo's name and my hand shot across the marbled countertop to snatch it at the same time Natalia started leaning over to look.

"Woah, what was *that* about?" She laughed, eyes widening. "It's the secret boyfriend who might have a one-hand-sized dick, isn't it?"

"Stop." I blushed, and my phone chimed again—another text from Angelo. My fingers itched to swipe it open.

"Answer it," she urged. "You're literally turning pink. I'm so invested."

I turned my back, opening the message out of her prying eyesight. "You're still being annoying."

It was a link to a new home listing outside Pompano, accompanied by a text.

ANGELO

Can we check this one out?

That was it. No hello, nothing flirty or charming. It wasn't personal, it was business. I bit the inside of my cheek hard. Stupid, stupid woman.

Stupid to be in a haze over last night while Angelo clearly couldn't care less. *Now* he wanted to be interested in viewing homes? This was the first time since we started working together he'd even sent a potential one.

Our not-a-date last night went so poorly that he was starting to do the real estate work himself to end it sooner.

I started typing, decided I didn't want to seem too on the ball, and deleted my message. Then I talked myself back into the professional mindset of being a quick and open communicator for my clients, and began another quick text that got cut off by the front door hurtling open.

Mateo strode in noisily, kicking off his boots and carrying two boxes of hot pizza down the short corridor into the kitchen. "Brought dinner, and a guest."

Angelo was strolling casually behind him with his nose in his cellphone and I pressed myself into the wall like I might melt into it and disappear. *Shit.* Shit, fuck, shit.

"Perfect," Natalia quipped. "Mia's here, too."

Angelo's attention whipped toward me, finding me standing there silently with my lips curled in on themselves, avoiding eye contact. I slipped my phone into my back pocket and cleared my throat. "Hi."

"Hey." The corner of his mouth curved upward.

"Sup, Mia." Mateo gave me a brotherly hug before scampering off toward my sister and kissing her very openly and enthusiastically. He leaned down to her belly and plopped a kiss there as well. "What have you two been doing?"

"Baby things," I answered. "I had some free time today and thought I'd start the spoils early."

"We were actually discussing how Mia's getting laid," Natalia blurted. "She's seeing someone."

A spike of red-hot embarrassment coiled from my head to my toes. Angelo tilted his neck, pressing me with a hard gaze and a confused eyebrow raise.

"I am *not*," I stuttered. "That is so not a thing, *at all*, and we should immediately stop talking about it."

Mateo put the pizza boxes on the kitchen counter and gave me an equally intrigued arch of his brow, following my panicked expression over to Angelo with an odd interest.

"He may or may not have a big dick. She's strangely confused about the size."

"I actually have to go," I proposed.

"Well you can't leave now," Angelo piped up, and after peering into his amused green eyes, I could *feel* the shade of pink my skin was taking on like a sunburn. "I'm interested."

"Leave the girl alone," Mateo said, then dialed back slightly with his attention on me. "I mean, was it too dark to see it?"

"Yeah, was it too dark to see it?" Angelo repeated.

My mind was awash with a shame I'd never known possible.

"She swears she's not fucking anyone." Natalia sighed. "I think it has to be a real estate private equity guy or something, but if I can't get the details, you two definitely aren't getting any."

"Smartest thing you've said all day," I mumbled.

"Angelo, how is Mia?" she asked him. "Getting along?"

He looked away from me for the first time since coming into the house and undid the three small buttons at the top of his TechOps polo. "When she's satisfied with me," he said.

I laughed nervously, taking an awkward audit of the room and pressing a serious glare in his direction. My lips thinned while his widened in a grin.

"When he actually gives my listings the time of day," I corrected. "Doesn't just walk through with his hands in his pockets like I'm a tour guide at a history museum."

"That's pretty much your job, only with tiny heels and a big attitude."

"You wouldn't have to deal with it if you were more decisive."

"I think you're a little distracted by the private equity guy."

"So there *is* someone!" Natalia blurted.

I jammed my tongue into my cheek and pulled in a centering breath through my nose. Angelo's grin lengthened. He flipped open one of the steaming hot cardboard boxes of pizza and dragged a cheesy slice out of it.

"I really do have to leave," I said. "It's been a long day, and I still need to go through a pile of offers that came in today for one of my sellers."

"Take a slice for the road," Mateo offered, grabbing his own pizza and dropping onto the living room couch with it.

"I'll walk you out." Angelo came to my side. "Left something in my car anyway. Be right back."

"Love you!" Natalia shouted to me. "Keep me updated on the nursery decor."

It was seconds after we got outside the front door that Angelo's hand wrapped delicately around my wrist. I pulled it away nervously. "Are you trying to draw attention to us?"

"Are you seeing someone?"

"No, of course not," I said sharply.

"Just me?"

"I'm *not* seeing you." Angelo's car was parked in the driveway. He opened the driver's door and put us in the shelter behind it, sweeping a rogue strand of my hair behind my ear.

"Kiss me," he said.

"Are you crazy? Did you not hear what I just said about us getting caught?"

"We're alone. They're talking about boring, married things inside." He lifted my chin, thumb brushing the curve of it. "Kiss meeeee, Miaaaa." He dragged the syllables out playfully, whiningly.

I couldn't help the smirk twitching at my lip. "You don't deserve it. You called me a tour guide with an attitude."

His white teeth shined, and the dimples in his cheek deepened. "I didn't say I didn't love it."

My resolve withered and I pushed up onto my toes, pressing my mouth gently against his. He took more immediately, a hum of approval accompanying the slide of his tongue against mine. He quickly pulled my hips into his with one arm around my lower back and I gasped quietly into his open mouth.

"Wait." I pushed him back. "I'm mad at you."

"What else is new?" he said, leaning back in.

I pressed a finger to his lips. "You didn't say anything all day. After last night, nothing. Not a text, email...it's like you weren't even thinking about it. Then you send me a listing out of the blue while I've been overthinking this entire thing since the second I got home..."

"Does it feel like I haven't been thinking about it?" Angelo dragged my hand to the zipper of his pants, holding it firmly against a very warm, very hard erection. My pulse thumped, but I catalogued the thickness of him in my palm, suddenly too overwhelmed to think clearly about the brashness of the situation. "Is it big or is it small, Mia? You tell me."

My eyes fluttered closed slowly, then opened in a dazed blink and found his dark, fog-in-a-forest stare. "Big."

"Big," he repeated, nodding. "Did it ever occur to you that I was looking for reasons to text you for the last eight hours in a cramped, sweaty lockbox of a post office doing a security install? That there wasn't a second of time under my brother's constant watch that I could manage a message just to tell you how wrecked in the head I've been, wishing I could taste you again?"

A surge of need dialed straight to my center. It might have weakened my legs, but Angelo was still holding my waist, keeping me from falling over. "Really?"

"My best excuse was to send you that listing. Then you were here, and now it's impossible not to want to tell Mateo that something came up. I have to go, and take you somewhere quiet, where we can talk all you want about last night."

He let go of my hand and it dropped limply, though I wanted it right back where it was. "And why can't you?"

Angelo smiled, a brisk laugh shooting out of him. "Weren't you the one telling me I was being too obvious?"

Get it together, Mia. There was more to life than a little whisker burn from a hot guy while being cradled in his strong arms.

"You're right." I cleared my throat, reluctantly wiggling out of his hold. "I really do have to work on some things, anyway. Plus I'll do some research on that listing you sent me and reach out to the seller's agent for a viewing appointment. In the meantime, try not to text me while I'm at my sister's house. She was so close to noticing."

"You're my realtor. Am I not supposed to text you?"

"It's too risky."

Angelo tapped my forehead. "You're overthinking."

I pulled my lip into my mouth and he tugged it back out with his fingertip, then replaced his touch with a feverish kiss. I could kiss him all night, standing in the driveway with the sun setting behind us and the dog-day cicadas buzzing eagerly. But again, I was forced to push him away with a clipped laugh and a smile so persistent my cheeks were starting to ache with it. "Go back inside," I said. "Before they come looking."

Angelo closed his door with nothing in his hands and I realized there was never something he forgot in his car. "Make that appointment so I can see you again."

"When I can," I told him.

"Soon."

"Patience."

"All out of it, babe."

My eyes flared and I shot him a warning look, pressing a hushed finger to my lips.

Angelo copied me, flaring his eyes, backing away quietly toward the front door of Mateo and Natalia's house.

I would call that seller's agent on the car ride home. Definitely.

chapter eleven

Angelo

WE WERE within a week of the one-month deadline I'd been imposed for finding a house. Part of me didn't think my parents would actually kick me out if I didn't settle on something. The other part was reminded of it very clearly, when I woke up Tuesday morning and my father was taking pictures of some of my bigger belongings and listing them for sale on Facebook Marketplace.

My commuter bike, for example. No, I never rode it, but it was one of those things where you didn't ever need it until you got rid of it. I wasn't a hoarder or anything. But sometimes a record player comes in handy. The mirage of items I fit on the trailer that I hitched from New York to Florida was my business, and my business only.

I had to wrestle the musical keyboard out of my father's strangely strong arms for a man in his mid-sixties and hide it under the seat in the cab of my truck.

This all to say, it was apparent that my time was coming to an end living in a basement or a spare room with my parents and comfortably allowing life to give me its all.

I was ready. I had been ready for years, but with the cost of living in New York City it simply didn't make any sense to go somewhere else. I was single, had a great job, a loving family, a space of my own, and even a side door to come and go out of. It was pretty much an apartment, without the bills involved. Economically, I was raking it in. Here in Florida though, my living arrangements weren't the same. The spare room with the flowery curtains and closet full of extra linens didn't exactly scream independence. Neither did living out of a couple open suitcases and a dryer. More than that, I had nowhere to bring Mia.

That was the *real* issue. I had nowhere to get her alone, to relax with her, to be in our own space, uninterrupted. Especially not while we were keeping a low profile. It was torture, not being able to whisk her away somewhere and touch her, kiss her, make her forget the world around us for a little while and make her *mine*.

Sure, we could fuck in the cab of my truck. We could fuck in an empty parking lot. I could get a hotel for a night, or I could invite myself over to her place and take care of her, but that wasn't good enough.

My feelings were more real than that.

Mateo gave me a day to catch up on my online classes while he "worked from home." Which could mean exactly that, or my brother was cranking his hog on camera for his other acclaimed gig.

I didn't ask about that side of his life often, but I did think about how convenient it was that he was a cybersecurity specialist given the nature of it.

Mia was indisposed all day. She'd texted me early in the morning to let me know she would be gone for a few hours taking listing photos of a property in Golden Beach for a wealth advisor who was selling his third home. That she expected it to go for more than eight million, and it would put her well above the second-best agent at Branting for the yearly sales report, given the fourth quarter went as well as the third.

It was hard not to be impressed by her. I guess it was a tough reality for some men to be involved with women more successful than them, more esteemed, better earning, whatever. Not me. Being with Mia would be the proudest brag of my life.

My only crutch was not being able to talk to her for hours at a time. By three p.m., I'd logged my last online coursework for the week and went back outside in the yard with a beer and a toolbelt to finish my thank-you project.

The wood stain was damn near identical to the worn, worked coffee table at the center of Mia's living room. It would blend naturally with the plants, the shelves peeking out behind green shrubbery. I added soft copper hardware as hinges between pieces that had the ability to open and close toward the direction of the sunlight, and stacked several planks with macrame knot ties to optimize the space, like a ladder.

My parents' windows weren't the same size, but I was able to do a test run in the spare bedroom. I drilled carefully into studs, and filled the holes in the drywall with spackle before they returned home from their regular Tuesday shuffleboard at the neighborhood clubhouse.

I took a shower to wash off the stench of wood stain and sweat from the hundred-degree day. My fingernails were an alarming shade of puce, which is just as ugly a color as it was a word, and when I got out, there was a text waiting for me from Mia.

MIA

> It's late, but I finally got a hold of the property guy for the house after I left him about four messages. Pulled a few strings complaining about communication, and he said it's open whenever we want for the rest of the night. Sent me the code.

ME

> Meet you there?

MIA

> Give me an hour

:)

Valley Green Drive was an interesting choice of street name for a neighborhood that was nowhere near a valley, nor in any shape to call itself green while in so many various stages of construction.

Number 11 was also one of only two houses on the road. The other didn't have a roof yet. It was all cement foundation and framing wood, some tarps in the rock rubble driveway covering raw construction material. The one we were seeing was at least fully functioning from the outside.

As soon as I pulled into the driveway, the skies started to open up. For the first time, Mia was there waiting for me with a stack of paper covering her head like an umbrella, her short heels sinking into the gravel, a skirt hugging her hips and billowing at her knees, and a pink blouse lying unbuttoned to the center of her chest.

A crack of thunder rolled angrily and I jogged toward her, scooping her up quickly at the waist, sending her into a fit of giggles, then depositing us both at the front door. Mia rummaged for her cellphone to find the message with the code, fumbling it, the rain only getting more threatening and her makeshift awning of paper becoming more mâché by the second.

"Need some help?" I offered, amused.

She whined out a laugh, abandoning the paper and letting the rain fall onto her perfectly dry hair. It curled in an instant, little ringlets swirling at her temples, frizz collecting droplets. Her shirt became as soaked as mine and the material made it borderline transparent despite the soft floral pattern.

"*Dammit.*" Her fingers shook on the keypad that was collecting rain as well. I nudged her aside to take a turn with the code, still needing to enter the procession of numbers twice before it finally beeped and clicked open for us and I ushered Mia inside.

When the door closed, the slam echoed throughout the house.

"So." She clapped her hands together, rocking on the balls of her feet and looking around. The walls were barren, some painter's tape left behind on the bottom step of a winding staircase in front of us. It smelled like freshly laid sheetrock, chalky and nostalgic to me, but procedural to anyone else. The floor tile had been started, but not finished. There were boxes of it still set to the side. "At least we don't have to take our shoes off."

The rain thudded louder on the roof, and it was incredibly humid with the electricity and central air being turned off with no one living there. The house itself was enormous. It just wasn't finished.

"Tommy is the property owner. He said the plan was an entire street of houses to accompany the new golf course they laid out, but they got stuck waiting on permits too long, the initial contractors backed out, and they moved on to other projects in the development. This one is basically done, but the interior obviously needs to be finished. He figured the right person, at the right price, would come and do the work."

"I mean, turn on the water and the electric and it's a fine house as it is."

"You can't live in this house as it is." She rolled her eyes and put both hands on her hips. I noticed for the first time that I could make out the white lace bra beneath her wet blouse as the material clung to her skin.

"I could. This is all cosmetic. It's a project, sure, but nothing is keeping me from finishing a bedroom and a bathroom, getting the kitchen in working condition, and worrying about the details at a later date."

We walked into the kitchen. Dust had settled on countertops and across the ground, but the wood flooring was new, solid. Cabinets were installed, alongside a deep stainless-steel basin sink. In the living room was a sunken area for eventual couches and a huge wood burning fireplace with none of those sharp corners and stone I hated around it.

More than that, there were windows from floor to ceiling, big and mighty, the main attraction in the house. Outside you could see grass as far and wild as it gets in the backyard, the property lined with orange trees that were littered with a crop that poked out in bright bursts through the gray and rain. It was a blank slate. Rife with magic and the possibility of everything I'd ever dreamed to fill it.

Mia and I stood there quietly, watching rain fall and splatter against the panes of glass, trickling down in a slow dance. "There's so much potential," I finally said.

She took a deep breath. "But why? I showed you houses that were move-in ready. Nothing to be done, completely state of the art, great neighborhoods with neighbors and canals. If you want a golf course, I can find you one. This is...it's a mess, Angelo."

"It's not a mess." I turned toward her. "It's a canvas. They need the right guy to do it, and I'm that guy."

"Can we at least see the second floor before we start imagining a building project? We don't even know if there's doors on the bedrooms. The listing conveniently left those photos out."

She led the way up the curving staircase to a long hallway of rooms, the main one at the end. There were, in fact, doors, a bathroom that shared space between two connecting bedrooms, and a third nicely sized one with an impressive walk-in closet.

There weren't machines, but there were laundry hookups in another space, conveniently located on the floor with all the bedrooms, and then double doors into the primary suite that Mia and I walked into last.

It was twice the size of the other bedrooms, with its own bathroom that had been mostly finished save for shower doors that looked like they'd need to be custom made, a deep jacuzzi bathtub, private dressing room into the closet, and a wall-to-wall vanity, still without a mirror above it.

There were large windows in the bedroom, too. Even skylights above the most natural place for the bed. Two French doors opened up to a small veranda above the living room with the same view of the backyard and the orange trees.

Mia watched outside curiously. I knew she could see the vision. The interior designer in her was brimming with it. She cracked the doors open slightly and a breeze whispered through on the tails of the storm. It washed a layer of humidity away instantly. "Perfect place for a late-night smoke break."

I came to stand beside her, treading softly. "I quit." Those words hadn't actually come out of my mouth yet. I hadn't even fully uttered the thought to myself. I knew I'd stopped reaching for a cigarette a couple weeks ago, right around the second time Mia told me how much she hated it, and I'd forgone the display at the gas station instead of buying another to replace my empty pack. "It's early days."

Mia blinked up at me, those big hazel eyes making me weak, her adorable wet hair now even more of a mane of natural curls framing her pretty jaw and perfect skin. I felt it in my chest, the need building, my heart pining after the woman in front of me.

"Why?" she asked faintly.

There was no use lying. Nothing to hide.

"I think you know why."

The air between us bloated. Her tongue darted out and perused her lips and she swallowed quietly. "Since when?"

My jaw flexed at the blanket of goosebumps rising over her chest and neck. The spring of blush I noticed always started right at her heart and wrapped like a vine around her throat and kissed her cheeks. "Since the second showing."

Her mouth parted and a short sigh came with it. I didn't care what I'd just admitted. That she'd been in control of me for far longer than I'd let on. That I'd been hanging on to the possibility of her for weeks, and if I were being honest, longer than that. Since Vegas, maybe. The first time Mateo and I had a conversation about me coming down to Florida to work for him. She was there then, and I wanted her then.

But I'd never wanted her more than I did right now.

I swept Mia's wet hair off her shoulder. "There's been other things keeping me occupied."

"Buying a house requires a certain level of focus," she said warmly. "Intention."

"I have a lot of intentions for this house."

"It's unfinished," she griped, watching me twirl a curl of her hair around my finger. "It's below budget, it's nothing like the homes I sell, and it's not even on my radar, which is why I didn't suggest a tour. It's been on the market for weeks."

"Like it was waiting for me to get here," I said, getting closer to her, close enough to inhale that light vanilla perfume, closer than an agent and a client should ever be. "Think about it, Mia. The potential is there. The framework and the bones of the house are all sound. It's big enough for a family, blank enough for personalization. The backyard is nice and open, private. There's no neighbors, but it's still tucked into a development. There's a deck, a terrace, massive windows for..." I stopped myself before I said something I actually wasn't ready to say. "I can make it happen. I can make it mine."

She shook her head, tugging her bottom lip between her teeth. She was taking a risk on me, I knew that. Who could guarantee that the entire deal wouldn't fall apart in negotiations, in the inspection, during any part of this?

"You're just a make-it-happen guy, right? A figure-it-out person. But how can you not care about the amount of work you're looking at going into this? I can find you something better."

I took her by the shoulders lightly, thumbs grazing the junction of her collarbones. Those goosebumps rose again under my touch. "The work is worth it, Mia. I like to work for things." She swayed lightly, her hands coming to rest on the front of my T-shirt near my belly button, her nails digging in slightly and making my stomach flex between pain and pleasure. "I like to *earn* things."

The room was dark with the storm still hammering steadily

and the sun falling lower below the line of trees. I didn't need light to trail my fingers from her shoulders down her chest slowly. Mia swallowed hard, letting me do it, not fighting the way I pulled apart the buttons holding her damp blouse together and spreading it open. The white lace bra was mesh and her perfectly hard nipples were taut against the fabric. "Don't you think you've made me earn this, Mia?" I crouched, nearly enough to take a knee, and slid my tongue across her breast. Her back arched, fingernails pushing past that pleasure and leaving marks on my skin I would revel at later.

I moved onto her other breast, sucking her nipple into my mouth, teasing it between my teeth and Mia's lips fell open, a sweet whimper echoing through the quiet room. "This is so unprofessional," she squeaked, but her hands dipped into my hair and held me close to her skin as I lapped at her.

"When you blush, it starts here," I said, kissing her chest, moving to her shoulder, the dip at the base of her throat, licking her rapidly beating pulse and then biting the lobe of her ear. "You get all pink and hot," I whispered. "I see it on your skin."

"I have keratosis pilaris," she argued lazily.

"You have a crush on me," I answered. "You know it's wrong. Just like this is." My lips slotted over hers for the first time all day and it was like a breath of fresh air, like being brought back to life. Our tongues mingled and she dragged my bottom lip between her teeth. "But it makes you fucking wet."

Mia's eyes glossed over. They were soft but not tired, feline in a way that gave me another jolt of interest below the belt. My dick pulsed heavy in my shorts, twitching for attention.

"Let's see if you blush down here, too." I fully dropped to my knees then, rucking her soft skirt up her legs until it was bunched around her waist and her panties were on display. I grabbed her leg and draped it over my shoulder.

"I'd lose my job if someone came up here..." Her words trailed off as I kissed the inside of her warm thigh and sucked on smooth flesh until a patch of crimson smarted there.

"No one's here," I continued, my nose nudging her legs open farther. Her hand landed in my hair again and I ran my tongue down her hip, stopping right before I could taste her the way I wanted to. "Can I eat you out, Mia?"

I looked up, into her lidded eyes. Her skirt was clenched in her fist, chest heaving, her blouse slipping carelessly off her arm. It was the closest thing to a Renaissance painting I'd ever seen. I'd put that in a frame on a wall any day of my life.

"Yeah." She nodded her head fervently, keeping my gaze as I dipped back between her legs and pulled the cotton panties to the side.

"Look how pretty you are," I murmured. Her cunt was puffy and wet. I blew a small gust of air over her clit and Mia's hips rocked toward it. "Tell me you're pretty."

"I'm pretty," she obliged breathlessly. A smile tightened my cheeks. I loved how gone she looked already, how needy, guiltless —it was all overcome by lust.

My tongue eased slowly into her core, teasing her bud of nerves, widening against every inch it could in slow laps. She tasted so fucking good, clean and tangy, warm in my mouth. I closed my eyes and devoured her, sucking, nibbling, holding her against my face as if I could drown in her.

Mia's breaths came louder, her hips grinding against my tongue in a rhythm that worked perfectly for the both of us. My tongue slid inside of her again, greedy for it, and Mia keeled over, curling in on herself with a long groan of pleasure. "I want you," she whined.

My eyes shot back to hers. I licked my lips, steadying my breathing. I'd gotten lost in her. My cock was throbbing, and those three words made it even more apparent.

"Yeah?"

Mia slid her leg off my shoulder and grabbed my shirt, tugging the neckline up and over my head. She was rushed, frantic, like she might change her mind if it didn't happen, and I snatched her skirt at the hips, pulling it along with her panties down to her ankles. "Are you sure?"

Mia dropped to her knees along with me and kissed me hard. I wrapped my arms around her small waist and explored, fingers creeping up her spine to the clasp of her bra that I pinched between my fingers and felt give.

Her mouth dragged across my jaw and neck. Another rush of arousal shot right to my dick, and the shudder of pleasure racked my teeth together. I was so fucking turned on it hurt. This was the limbo between torture and euphoria, the plane of existence where everything was tunnel vision. All I could see was her. Her hands sliding down my chest, through the hair there, across my stomach and pulling at my belt.

"I'm sure," she promised me, undoing the button, then the zipper. "I'm so sure."

Mia wrestled the band of my shorts down, along with my briefs until my cock sprang free. Her eyes settled on it hesitantly. She swallowed, entranced, and then ran her thumb from the bead of pre-cum at the tip down my shaft. My head rolled back with a grunt. "Christ."

She pumped her wrist slowly, kissing my chest, and I thought I might explode. Feeling her like that, all over my body, heat coiled in my abdomen. I was swelling in her hand with every glorious twist of her palm.

I had to be inside her.

She had the same thought, because she dropped from her knees to the floor, dragging me on top of her. Our lips crashed together and my hips notched between hers, grinding to find some friction against her warmth. My pulse pounded in my ears. "Are we about to do something stupid, Mia?"

She nodded. "Yes."

"You're going to let me fuck you?"

Mia squirmed beneath me, rubbing herself in small circles against the underside of my cock.

I sat up, reaching into the pocket of my shorts that were

pooled at my knees for a condom before kicking them all the way off. I tore at the foil with my teeth and rolled the rubber down my shaft.

"Do you just carry that around?" She giggled, though the sound tore away when I situated myself back onto her, running the head of my dick through her center slowly.

"I might have stopped on the way here," I confessed distractedly. My mind was elsewhere. It was at the tightness enveloping me, the inch by inch of her flesh wrapping around me as I pushed inside Mia Russo in the most gentlemanly way I could. Then, I hit a point of need so wanton it was like a pit opening in my lower stomach and I drove deep with a hard snap of my hips.

Her mouth fell open, a scream of complete satisfaction filling the empty room. Mia's legs wrapped around me as I thrust into her again, and again. Each pump of my hips earned an equally pleased whine of relief out of her. Sweat dripped from my temple. The room was a fog of humidity, heavy breathing, sex, a storm as perfect as the one outside.

"God, you feel so fucking good," I mumbled, pressing my forehead into her neck, grinding steadily as her hips came up to meet mine. "So tight, so beautiful. No wonder I'm losing my mind over you. It's never going to stop now that I've had this."

Mia purred, lips cresting into a smile. She pulled me up by the hair and we kissed. Kissed like we were starved, kissed until we had to come up for air and I could feel her arousal trickling around my cock.

"Fuck, you're going to make me cum," she whimpered. "Keep going."

That put me on the edge instantly. I rounded my hips, driving into her in long strokes and hiked her legs farther up my back, plunging deeper. We both let out equally devastating moans of pleasure. Her core tightened around my cock, small spasms fluttering, and I dipped down, taking her breast into my mouth again as I steeled myself to give her that orgasm before mine overcame me.

"Yes, Mia," I praised. "Good girl, baby. Good girl, let go for me."

Her back arched, fingers pressing into my skin, eyes shuttering closed. She squeezed hard around me, and my balls drew tight, no longer able to pull out all the way. I pulsed inside her at the same moment her legs started shaking and she cried out in breathless, clipped moans, like a wave had crashed through us both. It might have.

I thought I could hear her pulse beating outside her body while we lay there connected in the aftermath.

Mia collapsed limply onto the floor and pushed her hair off her face, taking deep breaths. I kissed her lips softly, her nose, then her forehead. She couldn't open her eyes but she was grinning nonetheless.

"My god." I pulled out with a grunt and she sucked in air through her teeth like soreness had already settled in. My skin was so slick with sweat I felt like I was wearing an extra layer. "Be nice if that shower worked right about now." I plopped down on my back beside her, rolled the condom off and tied it, realized there was no good place to put it, and flung it a few feet away. "Gonna need to redo the floors up here anyway."

Mia laughed wistfully, finally opening her eyes and looking toward me. "You're still set on this one? After all that convincing I just did?"

I found her hand on the floor beside mine and tangled our fingers together. "I want it," I said. "I know when I want something, and I need to have it now. I can't imagine anything else."

Mia twisted her lips, staring up at the ceiling, at the dark clouds in the skylights. Rain still pattered, though less aggressively against the glass. It was peaceful, serene. I wished quietly that we didn't have to get up off this floor, in this empty house, and go about life separately.

"As your realtor, I would advise against it," she said.

"As my Mia?"

She dropped her chin to her shoulder, staring into my eyes so intensely it felt like she could see through me. I brought our intertwined fingers to my lips and kissed the back of her hand.

"Then I'd say, go with your gut," she answered in a voice so small it was a whisper. "Do something stupid."

"I'm really good at that."

<h1 style="text-align:right">chapter twelve</h1>

Mia

BY EVERY CUT of the cloth, what Angelo and I had done was reprehensible.

As a real estate professional, I was appalled with myself. It was a clear breach of conduct, a nightmare of ethical standard. If Branting ever caught wind that I'd fucked a client on the bedroom floor of a new build during a private showing, I'd never work in luxury real estate again. It was career suicide.

Not to mention, it perpetuated all the worst stereotypes about women in my position. A sale hiking on the assumption that I might favor men in a sexual way, use my body to get ahead. Those end-of-year bonuses reliant on quarterly commissions would look like total mockery. Even when the reality couldn't be further from that. I had never slept with a client. Never went on a date with one. I steered clear of men like Scott because they were my close peers, and I kept my nose in my work to make sure a rumor couldn't even catch wind.

Angelo and I weren't your typical partnership in homebuying. Nor was I worried he'd go on to air out our little rendezvous to my coworkers. But I held myself to my own specific moral code. One I was shooting to hell every waking moment he and I were together. I'd lost focus and made room for something categorically lighter than climbing ladders and putting up numbers.

Now there was laughter, and playfulness, *hope*, excitement, a shred of danger that felt like fire in my chest. He had grown on me. Like English ivy climbing a trellis. I was being overtaken, because more and more of me wanted a future that included Angelo than a past that didn't.

I was meant to hate him forever. From a distance. It still might happen, once whatever high we were on inevitably crashed and burned. The problem was, one of us was going to have to be the adult here and end it. And after our night at Valley Green, I didn't know if I was strong enough to do it.

Tommy, the property owner, was thrilled when I sent a thoughtful offer letter over to him mid-morning. We'd gone in full price, contingent on those work permits passing through and nothing holding up the process for Angelo moving forward. I'd also made sure to mention how versed he was in contracting, that his entire background was in the construction business, and how he would take on the house in a way that would bring pride and class to the growing development. That he could see himself raising a family there, growing old there, becoming a staple at Valley Green.

ME

Offer has been submitted, and now we wait

ANGELO

How long do these things usually take?

ME

Really depends on the listing and the interest. Not sure there's been too much movement on this one specifically, but I left us plenty of room to negotiate

ANGELO

Would a cash offer help?

I pinched the bridge of my nose, gathering myself, but it was hard not to laugh at Angelo's pure neediness when he had his mind set.

ME

> Slow your roll, cowboy, what's meant to be will be

ANGELO

> Sometimes you just have to make things happen instead

ME

> I don't want to get your hopes up as a rule of mine, but I'm pretty sure you're sparring with a punching bag

ANGELO

> You're a rule breaker, Mia

Somehow, miles away, he could still make my cheeks burn hot and my mind go misty. The sex was unforgettable, the looping replay in my brain almost as good as the real thing. I was stuck there.

ME

> Last night was not my proudest day at work

ANGELO

> You did great

ME

> I'm rolling my eyes

ANGELO

> Pretty picture

I sent him the rolling eye emoji, though realistically my eyes were doing more of a flutter.

ANGELO

> Can I come and see you later? Mateo has me
> doing a catalog of our equipment, but I can't
> stop thinking about you

This felt nothing near casual, like it was meant to be. A secret that had snowballed so quickly from treading water to drowning. We *should* talk, face-to-face. That was probably the only way to get on the same page and stay there with the end of September, and the end of our working relationship, looming.

ME

> Come over after work

————

A FEW HOURS LATER, when I'd paced my house long enough to wear a mark into the floor, Angelo's truck pulled into the driveway in the space beside mine.

This time was different than the last time he was here. Then, it was reluctant and forced. We were still pretending the thing happening between us was fueled by mutual disdain. At least I was.

It was dark that night, but now it was daylight, and he bounded up the short stairs to the front door with a ray of afternoon sun following him. My stomach was in knots that seemed to tighten with nervous excitement. It was rudimentary. I was embarrassing myself and I was painfully aware of it.

The doorbell rang. I ruffled my hair in the foyer mirror before opening it, dragging him inside by the wrist and closing the door quickly. Angelo was holding a very large bag that he abandoned on the floor beside him, and I didn't even have time to ask what was inside before he was on me, stepping into my space, cradling my jaw in both his palms and kissing me desperately.

It was like syrup on already cinnamon-coated French toast, a dollop of ice cream with a slice of pie. Delicious on its own, but with a little bit extra to put you over the edge. His kiss demanded. It took, it stole whatever it could get away with. My back was pressed against the wall beside the front door, spine digging into the entry table. On it, the floral arrangement shook unsteadily and tore our attention toward it for the smallest second.

"I want you so much," he said, righting the vase before it could fall. His stubble was rough against my skin as he nudged my chin to the side and peppered his lips down my neck.

"Rough day at work?"

"Day, night," he mumbled. "Maybe I'm broken. I can't get you out of my head, not for a second, Mia."

My fingers ran down his tan arms, tracing a vein down to his rough hands keeping me caged against the table. "Maybe we're both broken, then."

"Wouldn't be so bad," he said, thoughtfully. "Another thing that makes this all make sense."

Our foreheads pressed together, eyelashes nearly brushing. This close, his eyes were golden, and he had freckles across his nose that had started to stand out in the Florida sun. I wanted to kiss each and every one of them, and I knew if I proposed the suggestion, Angelo would lie there for hours and let me.

"None of this makes sense," I offered plainly. "We're creating a mess for the sake of it."

"The sake of unbelievable sex," he said. "Some fun, some danger, atoning for the family."

"I'm sure this is exactly what they meant by *get along*," I chirped sarcastically. Angelo slid his hands up my waist, under the hem of my cotton T-shirt. I hadn't put on a bra, and he found my pert nipples with his touch, drawing circles lazily.

"No one could have predicted the woman sworn to humiliate me would be so sweet on my cock."

A buzz of pressure swept through my center. My heartbeat did a deep dive from chest to clit. I liked the way he spoke to me. An equal balance of praise and something edgier. It goaded me on.

I tugged his belt toward me, unfastening it until it hung at his waist. I was so confident with him. I didn't hesitate reaching inside his tight boxers, feeling his shaft harden in my hand before I took it out. His sigh of surprise only made it easier to lower onto my knees, cushioned by a very expensive throw rug, and wrap both my palms around his cock like I knew exactly what I was doing.

"Can I try something?" I drew my hands up and down slowly, eliciting a throaty groan from him.

"I might die if you don't."

Without thinking too long about the fact that my sister had been the one to suggest it, I lowered my mouth to the tip of Angelo's cock and sucked it softly. His eyes fluttered closed and he bit down on his knuckle. I worked both my hands in tandem with my throat, swallowing him as far as I could before my gag reflex started fighting back.

"I don't care how bad this sounds, I love you on your knees," he croaked. "You're a fucking picture, Mia." One of Angelo's hands wrapped into my hair, holding my head down for a prolonged second. I swallowed around the length of him, trying not to choke and he let go with a deep grunt of satisfaction.

Beads of tears pooled at my lash line, my lips stretched wide to accompany him, and I twisted both my fists, up and down, up and down, spurred on by every glance into his eyes being more blissed out and on the verge of orgasm than the last.

"What a fucking woman," he bit out. "Gonna make me cum inside that pretty mouth, Mia. Can I?"

"Mm-hmm," I hummed around him. His cock pulsed in my palms, and Angelo's free hand slammed hard against the wall above the entry table, holding himself up as he let out a harsh growl and spilled warmth down my throat.

Natalia would have been proud. I knew I was of myself. A man strung out on your performance and finishing fast was one of life's greatest compliments.

"Your turn," Angelo decided briskly, pulling me to my feet. I stopped him, wiping my wrist across my lips. He was insatiable. I wasn't much better, but we were still standing in the foyer of my condo. He hadn't even fully shed his work boots, and his chinos were pushed down just enough to give me access. This was a sordid display of intimacy at its basest level.

"Why don't you tell me what's in the bag, Jeffrey Dahmer?" I pointed to the large reusable shopping bag he'd left at the front door before mauling me.

"Fuck," he sighed out, catching his breath. "You almost made me forget why I came here."

Angelo picked up the bag and had me follow him up the stairs into the kitchen, dropping it carefully onto the marble island. I went for two glasses of water in the fridge and when I came back, there was a display of walnut woodwork on the table in what looked like stacked shelves. Some of the pieces were tied together intricately with knots of soft rope. There were hanging clasps, and metal hinges, a very clear pattern to the chaos he was showing me.

"I don't want you to freak out or anything, but I made this for you. For your plants." Angelo rubbed a hand down the back of his neck nervously, swaying from one heel to the other.

I didn't know what to say, what exactly was swirling in my gut. My chest tightened, but I was still acutely aware of the muscles in my face that were relaxed, happy.

"For my plants?" I asked.

"I would need to install it," he said, picking up the shelves carefully and taking each piece one by one to the lonely set of windows in my living room. "The idea is that you can use this like a lazy Susan, but hanging. There's layers that can stack against the window, but each one pulls in and out. More room for plants, and you can meet their individual needs for sunlight." He jingled a hanging chain on the underside of a wood panel. "This is a water catch, so if you put a bowl here for something like a pothos, you won't have to worry about the runoff dripping down and damaging the floor. The rope is functional for up to a hundred pounds, but also aesthetically pleasing. Selfishly, I thought it fit the vibe you have going on in your place."

Angelo lowered the shelves, folding them back into a travel size the best he could.

I was speechless.

He had made this for me. With his own two hands, and it wasn't a thing he could have possibly done in a day. This was planned. It was time, energy, a fucking labor of...something. It was a gesture far more intense and meaningful than I'd ever given him a reason for. More than I deserved.

There was quiet contemplation, and Angelo leaned against the table watching me process it.

"Say something, Mia."

I took a short breath. "What are we doing, Angelo?"

His eyebrows knitted together. "What are you talking about?"

"I mean this." I pointed at the shelves. "This is...it's not friendly. It's more than that. There's feelings involved. Real, actual, punch-in-the-gut feelings."

"Yeah, I thought that was obvious. To me it was, at least."

"We can't have feelings for each other," I jabbed. "You can't build me things, and kiss me like you do, and make me want more than I'm allowed to have."

Angelo's fists clenched then softened at the edge of the table. "Why the fuck not, Mia? Would it really be the end of the world to admit to yourself that we might be damn good together?"

"But it doesn't matter."

"Stop harping on what everyone on the outside might think about us," he said plainly. "Do what you want to do. Do something for yourself because you want to, not because you're expected to."

I laughed coldly. "What if it blows up in our faces?"

"What if it doesn't? I wouldn't be here right now if both of us didn't think it was worth a shot. It's a risk, you're right. I'm not born rich. I'm not a lawyer, or a doctor, or some fucking investment banker with girlfriends on business trips while you wait for me back home. What you see is what you get."

"You have it all figured out again." I swallowed hard to clear the emotion stuck at the base of my throat. He was right. He was right, he was *always* right, and he never sugarcoated it. He wouldn't let me out easily and I should have known that. I didn't want him to. I loved the fight, the sureness. "My parents will lose their minds if another daughter brings home a Duran, you understand that, right? They're still recovering from Mateo. My alcoholic father will relapse."

Angelo roped me in closer to him, lacing our fingers together. His eyes were dark, but determined. He pulled in a deep breath and let it go. "There you go worrying about other people again, Mia. Fighting it."

I bowed my head with an amused sigh. His thumb traced circles over the back of my hand. "It's not that easy for me to break a habit."

Angelo dragged his hand down his mouth and chin. "Well, imagine something for me. Picture us, without the secrets, or the sneaking around. Being able to go out to dinner together, experience things, make memories, actually *date*. If it doesn't look right to you, if you can't see it, you don't believe in it, then fine." His lips thinned. "After this week, house or not, we can call it. Never mention it again, never tell a soul what happened here."

I hated that option more than I'd ever hated Angelo. He tugged me forward, dropping onto a kitchen stool, me between his open legs, in too vulnerable a position for this conversation.

"We can pretend at family gatherings that I haven't been inside you," he murmured. "That I don't know what you taste like, and you haven't been on your knees in front of me begging for it." He ran his finger across my chin and I swatted it languidly. My lip trembled anyway.

"I don't know if I can do that," I admitted quietly.

"I sure as hell can't," he agreed. "I'm ready for whatever this is, Mia. I want to fight for it. I want to earn it. I'm here now. I'm not going back to New York, I'm not going to disappear from your life one day, and I'm not going to sit aside while you bring a Scott or a Brad or Chad home for the holidays just to save everyone else's fucking feelings. I won't let you."

I wouldn't let myself. There would be no comparison. I'd likely spend a lifetime looking for another Angelo and that person would never come. Then I'd truly lose myself to my job. Maybe adopt a few cats, volunteer more, embrace celibacy, start a club for objectophiles in a relationship with their vibrators. That future was glum.

Angelo was waiting for me to come to this conclusion verbally. He had a worry line etched between his eyes, his hands, clammy and persistent, holding me by the waist. I had his heart in my palms, and he was bleeding all over me.

My phone started ringing on the table, and we both looked toward it. I normally didn't save numbers, unless I knew I had a high likelihood of dealing with the person again, or needing it as a connection. However, I had saved Tommy's after the saga of getting a hold of him for Valley Green.

"I should probably take this," I told Angelo, eagerly. He let me wiggle away, and I swiped my phone off the table and walked into the far part of the living room before answering it.

"Tommy," I said brightly. "Is this good news?"

Crunching gravel and a tired engine whined in the background. "I'm calling to let you know we've decided to move forward with your client, Mr. Duran. We're accepting the offer for 11 Valley Green with the contingencies."

I smiled hard, pinching my eyes closed and pumping my fist in a silent celebration. "Excellent." I looked over my shoulder at Angelo at the kitchen table. He had a cool stare, tension in his neck, his long leg bouncing. "You get that to me in writing in the morning, and I'll start moving the pieces on my end. I expect there's not going to be too many hiccups on a property like this one, considering its...emptiness."

"You get someone out here for an inspection, and I don't see any reason we can't close by the new year."

"Thank you, Tommy," I sang. "We'll be in touch."

The call dropped and I stuck my phone in my pocket, turning on a heel and skipping back in Angelo's direction. He sat up straighter, still tense, confusion overwhelming the initial worry. I could see everything while he wore his heart on his sleeve.

I sympathized with him. It couldn't be easy sitting where he was in this moment. Hanging off the edge of his seat about his woman and his house, staring directly at the only person who had answers. I chose not to torture him anymore about either.

"You got it." I grinned, so wide and cheesy my cheeks hurt. "That was Tommy. He called to let me know your offer got accepted on 11 Valley Green."

Angelo's eyes widened, glistening. A sound of relief got caught in his throat and he stood, lifting me right off the kitchen floor into his arms, spinning me around wistfully. "Fuck, really?"

"Congratulations." My smile tapered into a fit of laughter as he spun me again. "We still have a lot more work to do," I added. "But I'm pretty damn good at my job."

He let out a hoot of excitement, placed me back on the floor, but cradled my cheek in his palm. Our foreheads dipped to press against each other. "Thank you, Mia. This was you."

"Technically, you found it. I was just a necessary tool."

"No, it was all you. You agreed to help me. You showed up, and kept showing up even when I left you with a busted taillight and in the middle of a street to catch an Uber. You stayed the course. I owe this to you."

My fingers ran down his jaw and over his bottom lip. "I wasn't exactly running away."

If this was wrong, what I was feeling—the elation, my heart doing flips, butterflies in my chest, *hope* for the first time looking at my future—then I wanted to keep being wrong.

"About before," I whispered. "I want to make us work, too. I think we're worth the mess."

Angelo's lips crashed down onto mine, like sealing a promise.

"But, I do also think that we should probably start small," I said breathlessly once we came up for air. "Maybe tell Mateo and Nat, and test the waters before diving in on the whole family."

"We can do that," he agreed, brushing strands of fallen hair in my face behind my ears. "Whatever pace you need. I want you to know that I'm not asking you to say that you love me, Mia."

I lifted my eyes to his. He was so serious, so warm, honey sweet. Everything felt secure.

"I'm just asking you to give yourself the chance to," he added.

Pressing onto my toes, I kissed him softly again. "I can do that."

Hope. That really was the perfect word for it.

chapter thirteen

"ALL RIGHT, so what if I do all the talking?"

The truck flew down Coastal, me in the passenger seat having a panic attack, Angelo driving with one hand on the wheel and the other on my thigh, as blasé as ever. "I'll structure the conversation in a way that doesn't feel like ripping off a Band-Aid."

"You don't think it'll be easier just to be real with them?"

"And say what, exactly?"

Angelo shrugged, eyes on the road. "We're having intercourse. And plan on continuing to have intercourse for the foreseeable future. Occasionally we may engage in cunnilingus, and fellatio."

I pressed my fingers to my temples. "Angelo, this is a big deal. How are you not freaking out? Your brother is a special forces veteran. He might actually kill you for disobeying his one strict order."

"Well he can't *kill* me," he snarked. "He needs me to help him code website security. It would be very detrimental to his business to off his only employee."

I clicked my tongue. Angelo's thumb grazed softly over my skin and he squeezed my knee supportively. We'd spent the night together at my condo, doing everything but sleeping, and decided first thing in the morning we'd drive over to Mateo and Natalia's house and tell them.

It would be a burden off our shoulders, even if their reaction wasn't what we hoped for. I was ready for that. I had run every possible scenario over and over again in my head in the shower, then during breakfast, while I sent some reply emails I'd received overnight. If any one of my sisters would understand this, it was Natalia. She'd fallen hard and fast for a Duran, and kept him to herself for nearly six months before bringing Mateo home to our family.

Camilla and Bella would be a much harder sell. But I believed in us, and I wanted to show Angelo that I was all in on making it work the way that he was.

If the relationship news didn't land, we would be at an impasse for the rest of our lives. There were a lot of awkward years at stake here. Taking this step really *was* a huge show of how serious we were about each other.

"You're my girl, right?" Angelo looked over at me. His hair was still damp from the shower, curling in a mop on his head, his short beard a bit longer than yesterday and a brightness in his green eyes.

"Your Mia," I said. My lips curled into a smile that matched his.

"Then that's all that matters," he said. "We're adults in a relationship. It happened very oddly, but organically, and we realized it was too good to pass on for the sake of logistics."

"And we did *try* not to," I pointed out.

Angelo shrugged, pulling into the busy neighborhood. Kids on their bikes raced beside us. There were people casting fishing lines into the man-made pond, and couples on golf carts rolling toward the clubhouse. "Eh, I didn't really."

"So then we can say you seduced me, that you were the bad influence, and I was—"

"Addicted to my charm, unable to help yourself, put under a romantic spell by the way I pronounce *caw-fee* and *hawt dawg*."

I snorted. "I was going to say, impressed by your perseverance."

He blew a dull raspberry. "Boring."

Mateo and Nat weren't expecting us. Well, not together, at least. Angelo had told him he was dropping by before work and suggested they carpool like usual. I walked in the front door behind him and my sister and her husband paused while eating breakfast, staring at us with genuine confusion and a flash of concern.

"Oh, hey, Mia." My sister looked at her cell phone with a raise of her brow. "Did you text me? I didn't see it."

"No." I laughed nervously, crossing my arms over my chest, swaying slightly and remaining in Angelo's shadow. "No, I didn't."

"Randomly got here at the same time?" Mateo proposed. He was at the window and pulled back the curtain slightly, looking outside. A grin tugged at his cheek.

"Is everything okay?" Nat asked, standing and walking over to me. She grabbed me lightly by the arms and gave me a once-over.

"Everything is fine," Angelo answered for me. "Perfect."

"Just thought we'd drop in and share some news," I said slowly. My pulse rang hard in my ears and I forgot everything I'd rehearsed all morning. The script had permanently disappeared, not even a starting point. My tongue went dry and I rolled it a few times in my mouth. I had never been this panicked, not even in front of a table of investors, or Mr. Branting himself. "Um...Angelo?" I gestured toward him, passing the torch before my voice began shaking.

"So much for being the one to do the talking," he whispered, bumping me with his hip playfully. I tugged my lips into my mouth and smothered another anxious laugh.

Mateo and Nat looked at each other, then back at us.

"Well, to start, I put in an offer on a house," Angelo said.

"That's great, bro," Mateo replied, smiling. "Proud of you."

"And it was accepted!" I boasted. "Last night."

"That's amazing, Ang!" Natalia congratulated him, giving him a small hug, then patted me on the back, too. "Are you so excited?"

"Thrilled, yeah. It's kind of a fixer-upper. But very big, lots of potential to really make it my own. It's all because of Mia," he quipped. "She's a ringer. Got it done quickly, and now I just have to convince Mom and Dad to extend my room at the inn until my closing, I guess. Technically, I did find a house in their month."

"We could always take you in for a bit," Natalia offered, and Mateo shot her a glare.

"Have you not learned your lesson about offering to host my family members?" he said. "We barely made it out alive last time."

"I mean, you could always stay with—" I stopped myself. "With...um, with Uber. It's like Uber Pool but called Uber Roommate now. You just look for a bed somewhere. Airbnb probably can similarly..." I tapered off breathily and Angelo's arm came down around my shoulders, bringing me closer to his side. "Can get you a place to rest temporarily."

Mateo squinted at us. "Is that what you guys did this morning? Uber...Pooled to our house in Angelo's truck at nine a.m.?"

A beat of red splashed across my cheeks.

"Gas prices are really high," I muttered.

"I also couldn't help but notice Angelo's wearing the same thing he had on yesterday, because there's a red sauce stain from my mother's spaghetti he ate for lunch on his shirt."

"Matty, why don't we just let them say it on their terms," Natalia suggested, and I shot her a look.

"Say what?" I gasped.

Natalia shrugged, grinning in a small, apologetic way. "I mean..."

"You *know*?"

"Of course we know," Mateo announced. "You're fucking."

"Woah, woah, we're not *fucking*," Angelo argued, holding out the hand that wasn't around me. "Well...we are fucking."

"*Angelo*." I nudged him in the ribs with my elbow, hard.

"We're not *just* fucking," he said quickly. "We're together. For real. Seeing each other exclusively. And we wanted you two to find out first, because you mean the world to us, and we know it will affect you more than anyone else, and that it might be better to ease some of our other family members into the idea slowly."

A breath was caught in my chest, held there stagnant and getting tighter and more aching every second that passed without a reaction from them. Angelo seemed more on edge, too. His fingers dug into my shoulder, his nostrils flaring when I chanced a look up.

Oh, God, this might be bad. This might be exactly what I feared would happen. And worse than anything else, I couldn't fathom losing the closeness I had with Natalia that we'd worked so hard on since her wedding.

My ribcage felt close to exploding with tension when she finally turned toward her husband with a jubilant expression and held out her hand. "*Ha*. Hand it over, baby!"

My chest deflated like a balloon being untied and Angelo and I both glanced at each other in shock as Mateo groaned and reached for his wallet in his back pocket.

He pulled out a crisp fifty and slapped it into his wife's hand. "How do you always fucking win?"

I tried to speak, but the words got caught, surprise reverberating through me.

"What the fuck is happening right now?" Angelo asked. His eyebrows had never more resembled a unibrow, smooshed together at the center of his forehead.

Natalia's smile was still stretching from ear to ear. "Of course we knew, silly."

"We saw you guys making out in the driveway last week. There are cameras everywhere outside this house, after a...learning experience with Mom and Dad," Mateo said.

"You didn't think to say anything to me?" I pressed Natalia. "How did you keep that to yourself?"

"This is sadistic." Angelo ran a hand down his face.

Natalia sat back in her chair, her hand on her little baby

bump. "We wanted you guys to figure it out first, and decide on your own when, or if, you ever told us."

Mateo leaned against the mantle of their fireplace. "We know a thing or two about being forced to bring things to light when you're not ready. We love you guys, too, and wanted to make sure that you told us on your own time."

"What was the fifty dollars for?" Angelo asked.

"I bet Mateo you were dating. Mateo thought it was just sex."

I scoffed. "I'm appalled. Wagering your sister's love life?"

"Haven't lost yet." She grinned. "We promise to keep your secret as long as you want us to."

"Please don't ruin Christmas," Mateo said pointedly. "Pike and O are coming back to visit and I'm begging for a stress-free holiday this year."

Angelo inched closer to me again, intertwining our fingers. I was so happy I was high with it. I smiled at him, and a giddy laugh shot out of me too. "We'll be on our best behavior."

"How did this even happen?" Mateo asked. "You hated the hell out of each other."

"I really tried to fight it," I admitted.

"I didn't," Angelo said.

"To be fair, I was also trying to keep my job."

"It was all that sexual tension in Vegas bound to boil over," Natalia said. "I'm taking full responsibility for setting this up, by the way. Look at how well everything worked out. A new house, a new relationship, I have fifty more dollars now than I did ten minutes ago, and an eternal bragging right to go with it."

"John and Sistine are going to take some serious work to be sold on this," I said to Natalia.

"Good thing you're an expert. Plus, they'll be preoccupied with a grandson anyway."

My eyes widened. "A grandson?"

"The Duran name lives on!" Angelo exclaimed proudly, crossing the room to put his older brother in a bear hug and kiss both his cheeks exuberantly. "Okay, new idea, what if we renamed the company Duran Duran *Duran*?"

"I'll have to sleep on that," Mateo said. "Forever."

"I have to start the nursery, yesterday," I gushed. "Oh my god, this news is a way bigger deal than what we had."

"Can I buy him his first baseball mitt?" Angelo asked. "Kid's a Yankees fan. I don't care if he's born here, we don't bend."

"You two are pretty perfect for each other," Natalia crooned. "It's a mystery we didn't see it sooner."

My heart was so full, it had to have tripled in size from the moment Angelo and I got thrust together into this arrangement. A month with my enemy turned into the possibility of forever with the greatest man I'd ever met. Maybe it wouldn't always feel this easy, this light, but I had a sense that it would always feel this destined.

We spent hours with our siblings, blowing off the day to brainstorm baby names and nursery plans. Angelo happily free-handed an entire blueprint of custom furniture I wanted to incorporate. By mid-afternoon, when we decided it was time to go, I'd all but forgotten the anxiety I started the day with. All my worries washed away, or, at least, were filed into a folder to be dealt with at a later date. But I wasn't scared anymore. What we were doing didn't feel wrong. It was the most intensely *right* thing I'd experienced.

It was hopeful.

It was inevitable.

We stopped outside the front door after we'd waved goodbye, and I turned back toward the house where Mateo and Nat were peeking through the curtains at us.

"Fuck off, creeps!" Angelo hollered, and the curtains flew closed.

It was breezy, less humid than the entire month had been so far, and the sky was perfectly clear. Angelo wrapped his arms around my waist and pulled me toward him. "That went surprisingly well."

A dug my teeth into my bottom lip to quiet the smile I'd been wearing all day. "I'd say."

He lifted a middle finger to the camera on the doorbell and leaned in, knocking his forehead into mine. Our noses brushed, my smile parted, and we kissed. With no one watching, with everyone watching. We kissed like we didn't care who might be.

He took me back to the truck, opening the passenger door for me. His arms hung there on the metal frame, closing me in as his shaggy hair blew gently in the breeze and his eyes gleamed like sea glass. So handsome, so incredibly mine.

"What's next?"

"I think we should go back to my place and you install those plant shelves," I suggested, tapping a finger against my lips until it broke into a toothy grin. "Maybe some *other* stuff."

Angelo helped me into my seat and stalled at the door with a triumphant smile.

"Yes, ma'am."

epilogue

Angelo

3 months later

11 VALLEY GREEN DRIVE looked the same as it did three months prior when I'd pulled into the driveway. Gravel under my tires, a mailbox that had never been touched sticking out of the front lawn. Grass had actually begun to sprout where it used to be only seed, and despite it being early January, I was still in a T-shirt and jeans because the weather came and went in cool fixes languidly.

I didn't know that I'd ever get used to the endless summer, but it beat being in a gray spell for months at a time in New York. Dirty snow piled on street corners, wind so chilly it could bite your ears off without a hat on.

Turned out I didn't have nearly as many things to bring to my new house as I thought. Everything I owned, my mother packed snug into several moving boxes as she stood over them with tears in her eyes. I swore, for a woman dead set on getting me out of her house, there was a lot of tugging and pulling going on as I hurried off to my closing. She was a true empty nester now, and it was hitting Anna harder than when Mateo left for the Army. Even with me only a quick fifteen-minute drive away.

I sat in my truck staring up at my place—the light siding, big windows, palm trees framing the front. There were a million things I still wanted to do. *Needed* to do. Years of work ahead of me adding my own touches to the landscaping leading up to the entry door, rocks to form the walking path, flowers and bushes, outdoor lighting. Inside, I would need the calvary before it was comfortable. My father and brother, finally doing the things my mother always wanted out of us as a crew, working together on building something meaningful. It just ended up being an in-house job. I didn't have couches or tables, no place to sit, not a bedframe or a towel to dry my hands on—yet. I was starting from square one.

None of that was important, though. What was important was that I was home. My truck in the driveway for the very first time with my name on the deed. The rightful owner, the one who had forever to make it all happen. And the woman to do it with.

A knock on the driver's window stole my attention, and an easy smile stretched across my face. Mia was there in her prettiest, most professional dress. It was all flowy sleeves and purple flowers, and her long hair was in its naturally voluminous state of curls. She looked like every dream I'd had since September, wrapped with a bow. She held up a set of house keys, jingling them excitedly.

I popped out of the truck, and my boots crunched the rocks under my feet.

"Welcome home," she said sweetly, dropping the keys into my open palm.

"It's been a pleasure working with you," I replied. "I'll let you know when I'm ready to buy that second home off the West Coast."

"Great." Her smile remained, but she took a step back. "I'll leave you to it then..."

I pounced on her, scooping my girlfriend into my arms and she laughed like a madwoman, curling her head into the crook of my neck. She stayed wrapped around me all the way to the door, as I fumbled with the keys one-handed and finally jammed them through the lock, passing through the threshold into my big empty house.

Empty only literally. My entire world was inside this house. She was in my arms, grinning at me with those gold-flecked eyes shimmering, her dimples burrowing as deep as they could go. I leaned down and kissed her, sweeping our tongues together innocently, and then not so innocently for a few minutes before Mia put a begrudging stop to it.

When I finally put her down, she went to the wall and made a show of flicking on a light switch that lit up the foyer.

"Let there be light," she announced. "We are fully operational, electricity flowing."

"Yeah, now I just need some flooring." I scraped the toe of my boot over the plywood. "A couple...hundred buckets of paint, who knows?"

"I specifically remember you saying you were the man for the job."

"Oh, I am," I agreed. "I think I might just need a woman counterpart for all those very intricate details."

We walked slowly into the kitchen, the big windows at the back of the house opening up to my favorite view of the orange trees in peak season, heavy and vibrant with fruit. Mia paused at the kitchen table and did a spin, looking around the space.

"This house would be amazing to design," she said. "But how are you so sure that what I would pick is what you would want?"

I shrugged. "I tend to like most things you do."

"What if I wanted a giant chandelier right here?" She pointed at the tall ceiling above the island.

"Then you should have a giant chandelier right there," I said, putting my hands in my pockets, happily observing her little tiptoe dance around the room.

"Maybe some patterned wallpaper behind the fireplace, sconces, mid-century modern artwork, cozy armchairs."

"You just tell me what to buy, sweetheart. You can call the

shots, but promise me one thing," I added. "Plants, for the windows. Those were always for you."

Her cheeks went pink, like her dress, and Mia folded her hands together still looking around, ideas swirling, that mind brewing with everything she could imagine this home being for me...for us, hopefully.

Mia and I were better than ever. As far as her job went, as of today, we were free to be completely open with our relationship. The closing marked an end to the client/realtor morality clause that I was completely on board with Mia adhering to when it came to her boss and coworkers. That didn't mean that we had kept our secret from everyone else as long, though.

By Halloween, her sisters were all in on it. We had a bit of an awkward conversation with Bella, who by lawyer standards was the equivalent to Mia in the all-stars of their work field. She'd metaphorically put me on the stand to figure out my intentions with her twin, and asked if my attraction to her sister meant I was also physically attracted to her, which would thereby disqualify me from being able to date Mia.

I had never been more scared of a woman, to be honest. I felt guilty of things I'd never even done by the end of it.

That said, they were welcoming and understanding. I believed my brother and Natalia fundamentally changed the way the Russo sisters operated amongst each other, and lucky for me, because with their acceptance, Mia was more open than ever to bringing our parents into the mix. We spent Thanksgiving with John and Sistine Russo, who took longer than they should have to recognize I was Mateo's brother, not just another man in South Florida with the same last name and likeness of their only son-in-law.

To be fair, they were aloof on their best days, and sobriety had strangely made John turn to long-distance cycling as a vice. Half the time we were away from the dinner table, he was urging me into clippable shoes to ride stationary bikes in one of their private gyms at the mansion.

Mateo had warned me, and I should have believed him.

Christmas rolled around and we spent it with my mom and dad, Mateo and my very pregnant sister-in-law, and Frankie and O, who had flown down to Florida in the midst of planning their own wedding for the approaching summer.

My mom loved Mia more than she loved me, and was thrilled to have another Russo girl under her roof, only regretting that she didn't have two more sons to finish the infinity stone of sibling matchmaking. But it was almost like Mia and Natalia were the female versions of Mateo and me, anyway. They were the daughters my parents never had.

I also hadn't been this emotionally close to my brother since we were kids. Now we worked together, lived down the road from one another, spent weekends with the girls, planned for the future while Mia decorated our nephew's nursery, and swapped stories untold from all those missing years apart. When he was in the Army and I was drunk on oysters in City Island.

Life was *good*. There was no ceiling keeping us from floating higher. It took until that moment, standing in my new house, with Mia sauntering, strategizing, making herself a permanent life inside mine, that it really hit me.

I was the goddamn luckiest man in the world.

"Can we color drench the bathroom down here?" Mia asked in her small, syrupy voice, as if she even had to run it by me.

"I have an idea for something we could do right now," I suggested, lifting her up on the kitchen counter and coming to stand between her legs.

A tiny gasp fell from her lips. "I'm fine with the change of subject," she mumbled.

"You can talk my ear off all night long about paint, trim, and pillows," I whispered, kissing her collarbone. "I love when you talk house-ish with me."

Mia hummed. "I love when you listen to me talking house-ish."

"But right now, I want to make love to my beautiful girlfriend in my brand-new house." I slid my hands down her thighs, lifting the long hem of her dress up to her hips. "We already ticked off the bedroom, but I think there's about nine more rooms in here left to christen."

"Ten," she said against my lips. "If you count the half bath."

"How could I forget the half bath?" I smiled into her kiss, rolling our bodies together softly, her hands threading into my hair. Every moment leading to this one suddenly felt like an inescapable fate. I was always worried nothing would work out for me, like I was bound to one thing, one life. It turned out the answer was in Florida the entire time, waiting. And her name was Mia. I needed the dots to connect, for us to meet, to hate each other, to fall for each other, before this day could exist.

Mia looked at me breathlessly and my heart melted. "Do you remember when you asked me to give myself a chance to love you?"

I nodded.

"Well, I do."

A broad smile broke across my face instantly. "I know you do," I told her, brushing her hair behind her ear. She dropped her forehead onto mine, blushing, releasing a small puff of amusement. "Took you long enough, baby."

"I needed to make sure you got the big house first before I could say anything," she joked.

A laugh shot out of me, and I kissed her with every emotion I was feeling all jammed sloppily into one. "I love you too, my Mia."

Her legs tightened around my waist, full lips curving.

"Now, come on. Give me one last house tour."

THE END

acknowledgments

My husband, my champion, my muse.

My kids for loving mommy and her wacky "computer job" and showing me why it's worth it everyday.

My family for anything and everything. Mom, Dad, Nan, Granda.

My brother, Tommy, who begged for a cameo in one of my books. There you go.

My novella sized moment at Hofstra in 2014 that changed my life forever.

My girls in the Safe Space.

Jackie Levan, because.

Makenna Albert, you make me refined and excited to do this more and more.

My hockey moms, for showing up for me and supporting me so wholeheartedly.

My readers for asking for Mia and Angelo and giving me this wonderful story.

also by karissa kinword

Read Mateo and Natalia's story in
FOR PLEASURE OR WORSE

Read Frankie and Ophelia's story in
CHRISTMAS IN COCONUT CREEK

For more visit karissakinwordwrites.com